His to Have

A Sweet Ranch Romance

Tia Marlee

A NOVEL CHOICE

A Novel Choice Press

Book Cover by Keele Publishing

Editing by Lia Huntington

Proofreading by Jammom Reads

Contents

CHAPTER ONE

Patty

Working the morning shift certainly has its perks. Having to get up before dawn isn't one of them. I slide on my non-skid shoes and head for the kitchen to grab my steaming mug of coffee. As I take a sip of my nectar of the morning, I glance over at my unmade bed and shrug. It can stay unmade—no one's going to be upset about it. Unlike when I was married.

My small studio apartment, above an elderly woman's garage, was heaven-sent when I rolled into Piney Brook a few months ago. At the time, I'd been thinking I'd go further west, but something about Piney Brook called to me. I fell in love with the small town's charm and stopped for a few days, then decided I'd stay for good. One morning, I stopped into the diner for breakfast and spread out the local paper on the table in front of me, circling jobs and rentals that I might get.

When Ms. Daisy saw what I was up to, she offered me a job on the spot. I swear she has a sixth sense about people in need. She didn't mind that I didn't have any experience, so I took her up on her offer. "We all start somewhere," she said. By the time I finished my first shift, she'd convinced her friend Ruth to lease me the studio space above her garage.

It was a far cry from the stuffy house I used to live in with Klive. I shiver and grab my keys. Getting away from Dixie Pass, Tennessee, and Klive, was the best decision I've ever made.

I step out of the apartment and close the door, locking it securely behind me. Taking the steps two at a time, I make it to the driveway in record time. I might not be late after all.

My light blue Honda Civic—the only possession I owned when I got married, and the only thing I left with—is waiting for me. I pat the hood as I walk out, then I swing open the door and slide inside. It's twenty years old, but the ole gal still runs perfectly. *Okay, maybe not perfectly*, I think as I start it and hear the whine of the belt I haven't had fixed yet. "Please, Gertie, just a while longer."

I pull out of the parking lot and head toward town. Of course I get stopped at both red lights between Ruth's house and Beats and Eats. By the time I park and make it inside to clock in, I'm five minutes late. I stick my things in the back, and tie on my apron. Time to get busy.

Several hours later we've made it through the breakfast rush, and most of the lunch rush. I've only got one table, and I'm grateful for the break.

"Order's up," Ricky calls from the kitchen.

I grab a tray and take the plates from the window, situating them so I won't drop them. "Thanks, Ricky," I say, sliding the tray onto one hand and balancing it with the other. I've worked at Beats and Eats for a few months now, and while it's harder than I expected, it's also a lot more fun than I could've imagined. Every day's as different as it is the same.

After the way I lived before . . . let's just say it's a nice change of pace. Though it did take me a few weeks to stop jumping every time Ricky yelled through to the servers.

Taking the tray of delicious-smelling food, I tread carefully around the corner of the counter and into the dining room. I stop at the table, balancing the tray on my arm. "A club sandwich, fries, and a side of ranch," I say, handing Gabby, my co-worker, her order. "And a BLT with a side of onion rings." I put Anne's plate in front of her and make a mental note to call her for an appointment to get my hair done. I'm overdue for a spruce-up, and her salon is the best in town. And not just because it's the only one in town.

"Thanks, Patty," Anne says, dipping an onion ring in Gabby's ranch. "When are you going to let me jazz up your hair?"

I laugh. "I am due for a trim," I say. "Just a trim, though. I'm not ready to go crazy."

She grins and points her half-eaten onion ring in my direction. "One of these days, we're busting you out of your shell."

I hear the bell near the door jingle and glance that way. Ms. Daisy's smiling from ear to ear and grabbing menus for the newcomers. "Don't look now," I whisper to the women who've slowly become my friends, "but there's a group of guys that just walked in that I haven't seen before." Fanning myself with my free hand, I add, "I don't think they're from around here." I wink at them both. Gabby's only got eyes for her ex, Heath, but Anne's been talking about finding love. "I'd for sure remember them."

Anne chews her bite of food and looks over her shoulder to where I motioned. She spins back around, covering her flushed face. "Oh my," she says, taking a sip of her pop.

3

"Told ya," I say, bumping my hip against the table before walking away to greet the men now comfortably seated in my section. If only I were as carefree and open to love as Anne. I sigh and clear my throat as I approach the table.

"Hi, there, gentlemen. What can I get you to drink?" Three of the men seated at the table share the same features. Dark brown hair, blue-green eyes, and matching smiles that could blind oncoming traffic. So, brothers, I'm guessing. The one closest to me has little dimple marks on his smoothly shaven cheeks. Swoon. The fourth man sports cropped blond hair and if he's related to the other three, I'd be surprised.

I listen as they rattle off their drink order—sweet teas all around—and grin. "I'll get those right out. My name's Patty, if you need anything."

Dimples winks. "Thanks, sugar." He jerks and leans down to rub his shin. "What was that for?"

The guy sitting across from him smirks. "You can't go around calling people 'sugar.'" He shakes his head. "That's a lawsuit waiting to happen."

I chuckle and shake my head. "'Sugar' is fine with me." I wink and instantly feel heat bloom in my cheeks. What's wrong with me? "Be right back with your drinks," I squeak out. Turning on my heel, I rush to the drink station and start filling cups with ice. My hands are shaking, and I'm debating dunking my face right into the ice bin.

Who winks at a customer?

A very handsome, drool-worthy customer, but still.

I groan. After my divorce from Klive, you'd think I'd have permanent blinders on.

"You gonna make those drinks or wait till the ice melts?" Ms. Daisy's voice startles me and I drop the cup I'm holding, scattering ice everywhere.

"I . . . I'm so sorry, I'll clean that up."

Ms. Daisy laughs. "Just finish making the drinks. I've got the mess." She grabs the broom and dustpan from in the corner and starts sweeping up the spill.

As I remake the glass I spilled and pour all the teas, Ms. Daisy says, "Listen, I know the Miller family. Those boys have been taught right and there's not a bad one in the bunch, so if you see one you like, you can't go wrong."

My mouth gapes open for a second as I stare at her, unable to retort. She grins, shrugs, and walks away, leaving me to try to get my head back in the game after that remark. I draw in and push out a deep breath, then put the drinks on a tray and make my way back to the waiting table. "Here we are," I say, carefully placing the drinks in front of them. "Sorry about the wait." I can't help myself, so I sneak a peek at their left hands. No wedding rings. Hmm.

"No problem, sugar." The man looks pointedly across the table, then turns back to me. "My name's Finn."

I blush. I can feel my cheeks burn with the increased blood flow. Drat having fair skin! "Hello, Finn, and who do you have joining you?" It seems silly to hold introductions, but I appreciate Finn's manners.

"These are two of my brothers, Caleb and Cooper." He points to the blonde. "And this here's Alec."

I smile at each one in turn. "Nice to meet you. Have y'all decided on what you're having?"

"What would you suggest?" he asks, his eyes holding mine a beat longer than necessary.

"I like just about everything here, but you can't go wrong with Ms. Daisy's fried chicken." It's true. I've tried nearly everything on the menu since working here, and it's all delicious, but the fried chicken's next level. "It comes with mac and cheese and green beans."

"Great," he says, laying the menu on the table. "That's what I'll have." His companions chime in, all asking for the same.

"Perfect," I say, tucking my notepad into my apron. "That should be right out."

"Take your time," Caleb says, leaning back in the chair. "We're in no hurry."

Cooper scoffs and says something I can't quite make out as I walk away. They sure are handsome, and did he say *two* of his brothers? How many men are running around in the world with those genes?

CHAPTER TWO

Finn

"So, Alec, Uncle Harry mentioned you've been managing most of the day-to-day operations lately," I say, watching as our cute server, Patty, walks away.

The younger man nods, taking a sip of his tea. "Yeah, been working there full time since I graduated from high school."

"You actually work now?" Cooper laughs. "I seem to remember when you were younger, you spent a lot of time just following us around every summer."

Alec grins. "Someone had to keep you city boys out of trouble."

"Speaking of following people around . . ." Caleb leans forward with a mischievous smile. "Heard from our sister lately?"

I watch as Alec's cheeks redden slightly. He's had a crush on Holly since they were teenagers, and my brothers and I have teased him about it since we found out.

"I . . . uh, I think Margaret mentioned she's doing well," he stammers, suddenly very interested in stirring his tea.

Cooper and Caleb exchange knowing looks while I shake my head. "Leave him alone, guys."

"Actually," Alec says, recovering quickly, "I'm surprised you all could make it on such short notice. Your uncle was worried you'd be too busy. He's grateful for the help, even if you two do need to head back soon," he says, pointing at my brothers.

I shrug and take a sip of the sweet tea Patty brought over. "It wasn't a problem. I had time off, and the ranch is special." My brothers pipe in with their own answers, but I'm too distracted by a beautiful brunette to care. My eyes find her across the room, rolling silverware. Her long chestnut hair's pulled up in a high ponytail. She flushed so easily when I called her "sugar" it made me want to do it again just to see her eyes sparkle and her cheeks turn that pretty shade of rose.

"Earth to Finn," Caleb says, waving a hand in front of my face. "You're staring."

"Sorry," I mutter. "What were we talking about?" I glance back at Patty as she jumps up to get our food from the kitchen window.

Cooper snickers. "He's too busy making eyes at the server."

"Can't blame him," Alec says with a grin. "She's pretty."

I scowl at him, causing my brothers to burst into laughter just as Patty reaches our table.

"Here we are," she says, setting the tray on a stand she's brought over. "Four fried chicken platters."

The smell of the chicken makes my mouth water. "If it tastes as good as it smells, I'm mighty glad about the recommendation." I wink at her, doing an internal happy dance when a blush stains her cheeks again.

"It tastes even better," she promises before gliding away to check on her other tables.

"Stop drooling," Cooper says, pointing a drumstick in my direction. "Or at least drool over this chicken instead. It's so good!"

I take a bite of the steaming chicken and groan. "You're not wrong," I say, licking my lips and going in for another bite.

We eat in companionable silence for a while before Cooper leans back and rubs his stomach. "Best fried chicken I've had in a long time."

"You should learn to cook," Caleb says, pointing a fork loaded with mac and cheese at Cooper. "Then you wouldn't have to eat out all the time."

"Nah, eating out is how I find all the pretty ladies," Cooper says, causing us all to laugh.

Just then, Patty returns to the table, our check in her hand. "Anything else I can get y'all?" she asks, placing the check in the middle of the table.

"Your number," I say before I can stop myself. Her mouth drops open in a perfect "O" and her neck flushes that pretty pink once more. I think I'm addicted to making her blush. Cooper kicks me under the table. "What's gotten into you?" I hear him mutter.

"I, um . . ." she hesitates. "How about you come back and see me again, and I'll think about it," she finally says.

Cooper laughs. "Smart woman."

Caleb elbows him and shakes his head. "Don't be rude."

Patty giggles, the sound landing straight in my chest. What is it about this woman that has me so smitten? "Sugar, you can count on it."

As we pay our bill and head for the door, Alec checks his watch. "We should head back. I need to make sure everything's done for the night and turn in. Ranch mornings come early, ya know."

Cooper and Caleb groan. I can't help but laugh at them. "Afraid of some hard work?" I tease.

"Nah, just afraid of dawn," Cooper says, pretending to shudder.

"I never get up before the sun if I can help it," Caleb adds.

Watching Patty clear our table as we leave, I can't help but feel a sense of possibility in the air. Uncle Harry found love when he least expected it, discovering his happiness later in life. This weekend, we'll celebrate their wedding, but I'm already thinking about when I can return to Beats and Eats. There's a quality about Patty that makes me want to know more—a lot more.

That night after dinner, Uncle Harry calls a family meeting.

Which basically means he stands on the porch and hollers loud enough to rattle the windows. In minutes, the three of us are gathered around the long kitchen table—me, Caleb, and Cooper—mugs of coffee in hand, the scent of Margaret's peach cobbler still in the air.

Harry stands near the stove, arms crossed, looking every bit like a man who's already made up his mind.

"Boys," he starts, "it's time."

Caleb raises a brow. "Time for what?"

"For me to step down. Margaret and I have been talking. We're moving to Florida after the season's over."

Cooper nearly chokes on his drink. "You're what?"

Uncle Harry's mouth twitches. "We're not getting any younger. We want time to rest, enjoy the warmth, maybe do a little fishing. And I'm too tired to run an orchard this size year-round."

"You're serious?" Caleb asks.

Uncle Harry nods. "As a frost warning in October."

"Wow," Caleb murmurs. "End of an era."

"I've been starting the paperwork," Harry continues. "Planning to hand the operation over before the new year. The orchard needs new leadership. Someone with skin in the game and better knees."

The silence stretches until Caleb finally says, "Then I don't think there's much to talk about. It's Finn's."

"I second that," Cooper agrees. "He's always dreamed of taking it over one day. He's the one who convinced us to come back and get things settled for the harvest season. Finn's been working with Alec—coordinating crews, solving shipping issues, and running the numbers. He's already doing the job."

"Yeah," Cooper says. "It's what he's always worked for."

I open my mouth to protest, but Harry raises a hand.

"I agree," he says, looking straight at me. "You've stepped up, Finn. More than I expected. But there's something important you need to know."

Of course there is.

Harry takes a deep breath, glancing at each of us in turn. "I've been thinking long and hard about this decision, and I've decided that whoever takes over this ranch needs to be settled. Married. A ranch this size shouldn't be run by someone alone."

Caleb's brow furrows. "Why would you require that? *You* did it alone."

Uncle Harry's expression grows distant, almost sad. "Because I know what it's like to run this place alone for forty years. The long days, the endless work, coming home to an empty house night after night." He looks at Margaret with such tenderness it makes my chest tight. "I found love late in life, and it changed everything. I don't want any of you boys to spend the best years of your lives the way I did, thinking work is enough."

"But Uncle Harry—" I start.

He holds up a hand. "A ranch can consume you if you let it. Without someone to share the load, to remind you there's more to life than cattle and crops, you lose yourself."

"And if Finn's not married on time?" Cooper asks.

"Then I'd rather he find his happiness elsewhere," Uncle Harry replies quietly. "I love this ranch, but I love you boys more. If none of you can find someone to share this life with, then maybe it's time for the ranch to go to a family that will appreciate it together."

The weight of those words lands hard.

"I'm not married," I say, though it's obvious.

"And none of us are, either," Cooper points out. "So . . . what do we do?"

"I don't want to marry someone just because I have to," I say. "That's not fair to them. Or me."

"I'm not asking you to trick anyone," Harry says gently. "But life's meant to be shared, Finn. I spent too many years thinking the ranch was enough, that work could fill the empty spaces." He glances toward Margaret. "I was wrong. I want better for you boys. I want you to find what I found with Margaret."

Cooper leans back with a grin. "So what you're saying is—we've got ourselves a Hallmark situation."

I groan. "Don't start." Growing up, Cooper would sit and watch those cheesy movies with Maggie every Christmas, especially after her husband died.

"You've got the ranch," he says, ticking off fingers. "The looming deadline. All you need's a small-town girl with a guarded heart and excellent pie crust."

"Shut up, Cooper," I mutter, though a grin pulls at the corners of my mouth.

"I'm just saying," he continues, "there's probably a perfectly good woman in Piney Brook who'd marry you for free apples and a front porch swing." He shudders.

Caleb chuckles, then sobers. "All joking aside, what are you going to do?"

I glance down at the table, thinking of a waitress with chestnut hair and kind eyes.

"I don't know," I say honestly. "It's a lot."

"You don't have to decide tonight," Harry says. "But I want an answer within three months. After that . . ." He shrugs. "I'll need to make other arrangements."

The soft glow of string lights brightens up the backyard of the old farmhouse, casting a warm glow over the celebration. Ruby, Maggie's daughter, outdid herself with the ceremony decorations. Several tables are spread out across the lawn, each topped with mason jars filled with wildflowers. A small dance floor's set up near the barn, where locals are busy two-stepping the evening away.

I lean against the wooden fence, nursing a sweet tea, and watch my uncle twirl his new wife around the dance floor. Margaret's laughter carries across the yard as Uncle Harry dips her dramatically. It's good to see him happy. Especially since he's been single our whole lives.

"You're deep in thought," Cooper says, walking up to me, two fresh drinks in hand. He offers one to me.

"Thanks." I accept the cup and take a swig. "Just thinking about how happy Uncle Harry looks."

"Yeah, it's nice." Cooper clinks his glass against mine. "Who would've thought the old grump would find love at sixty-five?"

I chuckle. "Margaret's good for him."

"Speaking of good for someone . . ." Cooper waggles his eyebrows. "That woman at the diner seemed real sweet on you the other day."

Heat creeps up my neck. "Patty? Yeah, she seems nice."

"Nice?" Cooper snorts. "Brother, she was blushing harder than a tomato every time you called her 'sugar.' Which, by the way, I've never in my life heard you do before."

I can't help the smile that tugs at my lips. I think about how her eyes lit up when she smiled. How friendly she was, even though I got the impression she's shy.

"Maybe I'll stop by the diner again soon," I admit. "If Uncle Harry's serious about me taking over, I might be staying in Piney Brook permanently."

"You should definitely go before the week's out, get to know her better. It's not like you've got anything keeping you tied to Montana except a bunch of smelly cattle."

I punch his arm lightly. "Those 'smelly cattle' are my livelihood, thank you very much."

Before Cooper can respond, Uncle Harry's voice booms across the yard. "If I could have everyone's attention, please!"

The chatter dies down as all eyes turn to the center of the yard where Uncle Harry stands with his arm around Maggie's waist.

"First, Margaret and I want to thank you all for coming to celebrate with us today." He beams down at his bride. "And to our loved ones who've traveled to be here. Finding love at my age is a blessing I never expected."

Margaret leans up and kisses his cheek, eliciting a collective "aww" from the guests.

"Second," Uncle Harry continues, "I have an announcement to make." His eyes find mine across the yard. "Finn, can you come here, son?"

"As most of you know," Uncle Harry says, addressing the gathering, "I've run Apple Blossom Ranch for nearly forty years now. It's been my life's work, continuing what my father started."

I stand beside him, feeling the weight of every gaze on me, and the weight of our family meeting from earlier this week. The marriage requirement. The three-month deadline. My stomach tightens as I wonder if he's about to announce that in front of everyone.

"But these old bones aren't what they used to be." Uncle Harry chuckles, rubbing his knee. "Since Margaret and I are married now, and I'd like to spend more time with my beautiful wife, we've decided to move to Florida after the harvest season."

Murmurs ripple through the crowd, a mix of surprise and understanding.

"Which means," Uncle Harry continues, "it's time to pass the torch. I'm hopeful that my nephew Finn here will decide to take over the ranch and continue our family legacy."

Relief washes over me that he didn't mention the marriage clause publicly, but I can feel the weight of expectation from the crowd. This isn't quite the bombshell announcement I'd feared, but it still puts me on the spot.

"Uncle Harry's given me a lot to think about," I manage when he gestures for me to speak. "It's a big decision, but this place . . ." I look out over the sea of faces, many I've known since childhood. "This place means everything to our family."

Uncle Harry beams and raises his glass. "To new beginnings and family legacies!"

Everyone cheers and toasts. The band strikes up again, and as guests drift back into their conversations, I'm surrounded by well-wishers and people asking about my plans.

Cooper appears at my elbow with a fresh sweet tea. "Lucky he didn't mention your forced nuptials," he says quietly. "Though you know everyone's going to be watching to see what you decide."

"Tell me about it," I mutter, scanning the crowd. "Three months feels like no time at all."

"Speaking of time," Caleb joins us, grinning, "you might want to get back to that diner sooner rather than later. Can't meet your future wife if you're hiding out here at the ranch."

"Subtle, Caleb. Real subtle."

"Hey, I'm just saying—clock's ticking," Cooper adds with a smirk. "And from what we saw the other day, that waitress seemed pretty interested."

I feel heat rise in my neck. "Her name's Patty. And you're both impossible."

"Patty," Caleb repeats. "Nice name. Patty Miller would sound better, don't you think?"

I groan. "I'm walking away now."

"Think about it!" Cooper calls after me. "You've got harvest season to figure it out, but Uncle Harry seemed pretty serious about that timeline!"

As I mingle with other guests, accepting congratulations and fielding questions, my mind keeps drifting back to our family meeting. If I don't get married, Uncle Harry sells to a different family. The weight of it sits heavy in my chest, even as I smile and nod at neighbors wishing me well.

Patty's face drifts through my thoughts—her shy smile, how she blushed when I called her "sugar." Maybe my brothers aren't entirely wrong about making a move soon.

The rest of the evening, one thought circles through my head like a mantra: *Three months to find someone to share this life with, or lose my chance at the dream I've chased since childhood.*

CHAPTER THREE

Patty

The morning rush at Beats and Eats is in full swing, and I'm balancing three plates of pancakes and a side of bacon as I weave between tables. My feet already ache, and it's not even nine o'clock yet.

"Order up for table seven!" Ricky calls from the kitchen.

"Be right there," I answer, delivering my current load first. "Blueberry pancakes with extra syrup," I announce, setting the plate in front of an older gentleman who's been coming in with his wife every Thursday since I started working here. "And two short stacks with bacon on the side."

"Thank you, dear," Mrs. Peterson says, immediately reaching for the syrup dispenser. Her husband merely grunts, already cutting into his stack of pancakes.

"Anything else I can get you folks?"

"We're all set, honey," Mrs. Peterson assures me with a warm smile.

I hurry back to the counter to grab the order for table seven, my mind wandering as I move on autopilot. It's been a few days since that handsome stranger—Finn—came in to the diner with his brothers and friend. My cheeks warm at the memory of him calling me "sugar" and asking for my number.

"Earth to Patty!" Ms. Daisy waves a hand in front of my face. "You've been staring at that syrup bottle for a full minute. You feeling all right?"

I blink, startled out of my thoughts. "Sorry, Ms. Daisy. Just a little tired this morning."

She gives me a knowing look that makes me wonder if my thoughts are written across my forehead like that scrolling sign in Times Square. "Mm-hmm. Tired from thinking about that handsome cowboy who had eyes for you the other day?"

I feel the heat rise in my cheeks. "I wasn't . . . I mean . . ."

Ms. Daisy laughs. "Honey, I've been running this diner for thirty years. I know that look when I see it."

"It's nothing," I insist, grabbing the plates for table seven.

"If you say so," Ms. Daisy says with a wink, clearly not believing me for a second.

I deliver the food to the table, take two more orders, and refill a half dozen coffee cups before the rush finally eases. By eleven, the breakfast crowd's thinned out, and I have a moment to breathe.

I'm wiping down the counter when Anne slides onto a stool.

"Coffee, please," she says dramatically. "Mrs. Winters wanted a complete color change at eight this morning. Eight! Who goes from brunette to blonde at that hour?"

I laugh, pouring her a cup. "Someone who's having a midlife crisis?"

"Exactly," Anne sighs, doctoring her coffee with cream and sugar. "So, any sign of your cowboy?"

I nearly drop the coffee pot. "He's not my mystery man."

"That's not what Gabby told me," Anne teases. "She said he couldn't take his eyes off you, and you were blushing like a schoolgirl. I kept trying to turn around, but Gabby insisted I not be a peeper." She scoffs.

"I hate small towns," I mutter, even though I don't mean it. The closeness of Piney Brook is what made me stay, after all. So different from the isolation I felt in my marriage. Klive's possessiveness kept me from forming any real friendships.

"No, you don't," Anne says confidently, taking a sip of her coffee. "You love it here, and you know it."

I smile. "You're right. But I don't love how everyone knows my business before I do."

"Speaking of business,"—Anne leans forward conspiratorially—"Ruth told me this morning that her arthritis is acting up again. She's been thinking of visiting her sister in Florida for a few weeks this winter."

"That sounds nice," I say. "The warm weather would probably be good for her joints."

"Exactly what I told her," Anne agrees.

I smile at the thought of Ruth enjoying the warm Florida sunshine. Ever since my grandma died, I've been alone. There's no family for me to visit, and for some reason, that makes my eyes start to water.

"Is everything okay?" Anne asks, concern etched on her face.

"Yeah, just thinking about the future," I say honestly.

"That's always a good thing to consider," Anne says with a knowing smile. "Especially when you've got a handsome rancher interested in you."

The bell above the door jingles, and I glance up automatically. My heart skips a beat as a familiar figure walks in.

Finn.

He's alone this time, dressed in a simple blue button-down that makes his eyes stand out and well-worn jeans that look like they were handmade just for him. He's even more handsome than I remembered. His eyes scan the diner, and when they land on me, his face breaks into a grin that makes my knees weak.

"Well, well," Anne murmurs into her coffee cup. "Speak of the devil."

"Shh," I hiss, smoothing my apron with suddenly trembling hands.

Ms. Daisy appears from the kitchen, menus in hand, but stops when she spots Finn. Her eyes dart to me, then back to him, and a knowing smile spreads across her face. "I've got some things to handle in the office," she announces. "Patty, would you mind seating that gentleman?"

"Real subtle," I mutter, earning a chuckle from Anne.

"I'll just take my coffee to go," Anne says, reaching over the counter for a styrofoam cup. "Wouldn't want to intrude." She dumps her coffee into the to-go cup, drops a five dollar bill on the counter, and winks at me as she heads to the front door. On her way out, she passes Finn, giving him a friendly nod that is both welcoming and slightly threatening.

Taking a deep breath, I grab a menu and make my way over to Finn, who's still standing by the entrance, looking far too good for someone who's just casually stopped by a diner.

"Welcome back to Beats and Eats," I say, aiming for professional, but hearing the slight quiver in my voice. "Just one today?"

"Just me," he confirms, his smile warming his entire face. "I was hoping you'd be working, today, sugar."

My stomach flutters. "Lucky you, I'm here nearly every day. Would you prefer a booth or the counter?" I ask, gesturing to the nearly empty dining room.

"Wherever you are," he says. "If that's okay? I was hoping to talk if you had some time between tables."

My curiosity piques. "The corner booth's usually pretty quiet," I suggest, leading him to the farthest table where we'd have some privacy. "Not that we're exactly slammed right now."

Finn slides into the booth, and I hand him the menu. "Can I get you a drink?"

"Sweet tea, please," he says.

"I'll be right back with that." I hurry back to the counter, feeling his eyes on me the whole way.

Ms. Daisy's waiting by the drink station with a knowing look on her wrinkled face. "Take your break, honey. It's slow, and that young man clearly didn't come in just for the food."

"Are you sure? I can—"

"Patty," Ms. Daisy interrupts, "life doesn't always give us second chances to talk to someone who makes our heart race. Take the break."

"Is it that obvious?" I whisper, mortified.

Ms. Daisy chuckles. "Only to someone who's seen as many love stories start in this diner as I have. Go on, I'll bring his sweet tea over."

I untie my apron with shaking hands and slip into the restroom to check my appearance. My ponytail is slightly messy from the morning rush, so I quickly smooth it down, then roll my eyes at myself in the mirror. "Get a grip, Patty," I mutter. "He's just a customer."

A customer who came back specifically to see me, a small voice in my head points out.

When I emerge, Ms. Daisy's already delivered Finn's sweet tea and is chatting with him about how long he plans to stay in town. She pats my shoulder as I approach, giving me an approving nod before heading back to the counter.

"Sorry about that," I say, sliding into the booth across from him.

"Don't be," Finn says. "Ms. Daisy was just telling me she makes the best sweet tea in Arkansas."

"She's right," I confirm. "Though I might be biased, since she gave me a job when I really needed one."

"How long have you worked here?" he asks, leaning forward slightly, his eyes focused on me with genuine interest.

"About nine months," I say. "I was just passing through Piney Brook, but everyone here was so nice it made me want to stay."

"I can understand that." He nods. "This town has a way of making you feel at home."

"You're from around here?" I ask, realizing I know almost nothing about him except that he has brothers and likes sweet tea and fried chicken.

"My family's ranch is about twenty minutes outside town—Apple Blossom Ranch. I grew up spending summers there, but I've been working in Montana the past few years."

"Apple Blossom Ranch," I repeat. "That sounds beautiful."

"It is," he says, a wistful expression crossing his face. "Especially in spring, when the orchards are in bloom."

"I'd love to see that someday," I say before I can stop myself.

Finn's eyes brighten. "Actually, that's part of why I came by today. I, uh . . . I wanted to ask you a question."

My pulse quickens. "Oh?"

"I'm staying in town for at least the next few months," he says. "Maybe longer. There's been some . . . family business to sort out."

"I hope everything's okay," I say, concerned by the hint of worry I catch in his voice.

"It's complicated," he says, running a hand through his hair. "But I was wondering if maybe you'd like to have dinner with me sometime? We could get to know each other better?"

My heart races. A date. He's asking me on a date. Part of me wants to say yes immediately, but another part—the part that still flinches at loud noises and checks the locks twice before bed—hesitates.

"I'd like that," I say cautiously. "But I should warn you, I'm not . . . I don't have the best track record with relationships."

Finn's expression softens. "Me either. Just dinner and friendly conversation. No pressure."

"No pressure," I repeat, liking the sound of that. "In that case, yes. I'd love to have dinner with you."

His smile's so bright it could light up the whole diner. "Great! When are you free?"

"I'm off tomorrow night," I tell him. "And Sunday."

"Tomorrow sounds perfect," he says. "I could pick you up at six?"

I hesitate. "How about I meet you somewhere instead?"

If he's offended by my caution, he doesn't show it. "Of course. There's a nice little Italian place in Barberville—Salvatore's. Have you been there?"

I shake my head. "Not yet, but I've heard good things."

"Six o'clock at Salvatore's, then," he confirms.

"I should get back to work," I say, reluctantly rising from the booth.

"Wait, can I get your number?" he asks.

I tear off an order slip and write my number on it before passing it over.

"Thanks, sugar," Finn says with a grin and a wink, then pushes to his feet. "I've got to run, but I'm looking forward to tomorrow night."

"Me too," I admit, surprised by how much I mean it.

I go back to work, helping the new table that's seated in my section, but I can't help but steal a glance at Finn as he slips out the front door after stopping at the register to pay for his tea. There's an openness from him that feels different. Safe.

But I've been wrong before.

"He's grown into quite a nice young man," Ms. Daisy says, joining me as I clear the used table.

"He seems like it," I agree.

"But you're still worried," she observes.

I sigh. "It's hard to trust my judgment again."

Ms. Daisy pats my hand gently. "The heart knows, Patty. And from what I can see, yours has been through enough to recognize the difference between a wolf and a good man."

"I hope so," I murmur.

The rest of my shift passes in a blur of coffee refills and lunch orders, but my mind keeps drifting to tomorrow night. A date. My first since leaving Klive.

As I'm hanging up my apron at the end of my shift, Anne bursts through the door, eyes wide with excitement.

"Well?" she demands.

I laugh. "Don't you have a hair salon to run?"

Anne rolls her eyes. "Lainey's working. I get off early on Thursdays. Besides, I couldn't wait to see what happened with you and Mr. Tall, Dark, and Handsome."

"Well," I say, pausing to drag out the suspense. "He asked me to dinner tomorrow night."

Anne squeals. "I knew it! Where's he taking you? What are you wearing? Do you need to borrow my black heels?"

"Slow down," I say, raising my hands in surrender. "It's just dinner at Salvatore's. Nothing too fancy."

"Nothing too fancy?" Anne looks scandalized. "Honey, this is your first date since you moved to Piney Brook. It's a big deal!"

I laugh, brushing her off, but her words replay in the back of my mind as we say our goodbyes and I clock out.

As I drive home, I find myself humming along to the radio. A date with Finn, friends who care about me, and a job I enjoy. Life in Piney Brook keeps getting better.

Ruth's working in her small front garden when I pull in. She waves as I approach. "You look happy," she says, brushing dirt from her hands.

"I am," I say, surprised by how true it feels. "I have a date tomorrow night."

"With that handsome young man from the ranch?" Ruth asks, a knowing smile on her face.

"How did you . . . ? Never mind," I laugh. "Small town."

"The smallest," Ruth agrees. "I'm happy for you dear. You deserve good things."

For the first time in a long while, I'm starting to believe that might be true.

CHAPTER FOUR

Finn

I arrive at Salvatore's twenty minutes early, too nervous to sit around at the ranch any longer. Uncle Harry raised an eyebrow when I mentioned having dinner in town, and Cooper smirked knowingly when I borrowed his aftershave. Some things never change, even when you're pushing thirty.

The restaurant is cozy, with checkered tablecloths and Italian music playing softly in the background. A few couples are already seated, enjoying their meals by candlelight. I give my name to the hostess, who leads me to the corner table I requested when making the reservation.

"Can I get you a drink while you wait for your date?" she asks with a friendly smile.

"I'd rather wait, thanks," I reply, not wanting to start without Patty.

As I wait, I fidget with the napkin. What am I doing here? I hardly know this woman, and yet I can't stop thinking about her. Under normal circumstances, I'd be excited about a first date, taking my time to see where things might lead.

But these aren't normal circumstances. So much is up in the air. The ticking clock of the three-month deadline looms over everything.

I'm watching another couple get their food, then turn to look as the front door opens, and Patty walks in. My breath catches. She's wearing a simple blue dress and her hair is loose around her shoulders instead of the usual ponytail she sports at the diner. She looks beautiful, but also a little nervous as she scans the restaurant.

I stand as she approaches, and her face relaxes into a smile when she sees me.

"Hi," she says, slightly breathless. "Sorry I'm late."

"You're right on time," I assure her, pulling out my chair. "You look beautiful."

A blush colors her cheeks. "Thank you. You clean up pretty nice yourself."

Once she's seated, I settle across from her, suddenly tongue-tied despite having rehearsed some conversation starters on the drive over.

"I've never been here before," she says, looking around. "It's charming."

"The food's amazing," I tell her, grateful for the easy topic. "The owner, Mr. Salvatore, moved here from Italy when I was a kid. Everything's made from scratch."

As if on cue, an older gentleman with a thick Italian accent approaches our table. "Finn! It's been too long!"

I stand to shake his hand. "Mr. Salvatore, great to see you too. This is Patty."

"Ah, what a beautiful signora," he says with a warm smile, turning to Patty. "Any friend of Finn's is a friend of mine. I will bring you my special appetizers, on the house."

"That's very kind," Patty says, "but you don't have to—"

"No arguments," Mr. Salvatore insists, waving a hand dismissively. "You enjoy, yes? I take care of everything." With that, he bustles away toward the kitchen.

"Friend of yours?" she asks with an amused smile.

"My uncle Harry's been coming here since they opened," I explain. "We used to eat here every week during my summer visits."

"Where'd you grow up?" she asks.

"My dad moved us to Chicago for work when I was young. But we spent every summer at Apple Blossom Ranch. It was like having two different lives."

"That sounds nice," she says. "Having both experiences, I mean. I grew up in the same small town my whole life until . . ." She trails off, sadness flickering in her eyes before she changes the subject. "What made you decide to work in Montana instead of staying at your family's ranch?"

"I wanted to prove to myself I had what it takes to work a ranch," I explain. "Apple Blossom is primarily orchards and crops. I figured I could learn different skills elsewhere, then bring that knowledge back someday."

"And now someday's here sooner than you expected," she says. "I overheard some ladies talking about Harry's retirement at the diner."

"Yeah," I admit. "Uncle Harry's retirement caught me off guard. He's always been this strong, tireless cowboy. Never slows down. First one up in the mornings. It's weird to think of him as old."

A server arrives with two glasses of water and a platter of antipasto. "Compliments of Mr. Salvatore," she says, setting everything on the table before leaving us to our conversation.

"Is taking over the ranch what you want?" Patty asks, taking a piece of cheese from the platter.

"It is. I've always loved the place, and the thought of continuing a family legacy." I take a sip of my water. "What about you? Did you always want to be a waitress?"

Patty laughs, the sound light and surprisingly full. "Hardly. I sort of fell into it when I came to Piney Brook. Ms. Daisy took a chance on me despite my lack of experience."

"What did you do before?" I ask.

She hesitates. "I was married," she says finally. "I didn't work. Though at one time, I was in school for business management."

The careful way she phrases it makes me wonder what she's not saying. "And now you're . . . not married?" I don't think she'd be here with me if she was, but these days you have to ask.

"No, I'm not," she confirms, meeting my eyes directly. "I'm divorced. It wasn't a good situation."

The tightness in her voice tells me there's a lot to the story, but her expression makes it clear she's not ready to talk about it.

"I'm sorry to hear that," I say simply.

She gives me a small, grateful smile. "It's in the past. I'm focused on building a new life now. Creating my own happiness."

"In Piney Brook?"

"That's the plan," she says.

Our server returns to take our orders—chicken parmesan for Patty, lasagna for me—and the conversation shifts to lighter topics. I learn that she loves to garden but hasn't had space for it at her apartment. She tells me about her friendship with Anne and Gabby, and how Ms. Daisy's like a mother to her.

I share stories about growing up with my brothers, our summers at the ranch, and my work in Montana. It's easy talking to Patty. Unlike the women I've dated in the past, she seems genuine. I've even gotten her to laugh—really laugh—a couple of times, and the sound of it made me want more. By the time we finish our meals, I feel like I've known her much longer than just a few days.

"Dessert?" I offer when the server returns to clear our plates.

"I couldn't eat another bite," she says, leaning back in her chair. "Everything was delicious."

"At least let me get you a coffee?" I ask, not ready for the night to end.

She smiles. "Coffee sounds perfect."

While we wait for our coffees, I find myself staring at her more than is probably polite. She's captivated me. She's beautiful, yes, but it's more than that. There's a quiet strength beneath her gentleness that draws me in. She's been through a lot, that much is clear, but she hasn't let it harden her.

"You're staring," she points out softly, breaking me out of my thoughts.

"Sorry," I say, feeling heat rise in my cheeks. "I was just thinking that I'm really glad I came back to the diner to see you."

Her smile reaches her eyes. "I'm glad you did too."

Our coffees arrive, and as we sip them, I find myself wishing the evening wouldn't end.

"I should probably get going," she says, glancing at her watch. "Early shift tomorrow."

"Of course," I nod, signaling for the check. When it arrives, I quickly pay despite Patty's protests.

"Next time can be your treat," I suggest, then immediately wonder if I'm being presumptuous.

Patty smiles. "I'd like that."

I walk her to her car—a worn but clean Honda parked a block from the restaurant. The evening air's cool, and when she shivers slightly, I resist the urge to put my arm around her shoulders.

"I had a really nice time tonight," she says when we reach her car.

"Me too," I reply, suddenly feeling like a teenager again, unsure if I should try for a goodnight kiss.

Patty solves my dilemma by raising up on her tiptoes and placing a soft kiss on my cheek. "Goodnight, Finn."

"Goodnight, Patty," I say, too surprised to say anything more clever.

I watch as she gets into her car and drives away, my hand unconsciously touching the spot where her lips brushed my skin.

The drive back to Apple Blossom Ranch gives me plenty of time to think about our evening. I like Patty. A lot. But the reality of my situation dims some of the excitement from our first date.

Three months. That's all the time I have to figure out a solution to Uncle Harry's stipulation, or watch the ranch I love get sold to another family.

Alec's still up when I get home, sitting on the porch with a sweet tea in hand and paperwork spread out on the table beside him.

"How was your date?" he asks as I climb the steps.

"Word travels fast," I say, taking a seat beside him.

He chuckles. "Mr. Salvatore called Margaret to say you were having dinner with a pretty girl."

34

I groan. "Of course he did."

"So?" Alec prompts. "How was it?"

"Good," I admit. "Really good, actually."

"But?" Alec looks at me knowingly.

"But I have a three-month deadline hanging over my head," I sigh. "Not exactly the best circumstances for starting a relationship."

Alec grimaces. "Well, what did you think of her?"

"She's sweet. Intelligent. There's a quietness to her, but also a strength. She's been through a tough time, I think, though she didn't share details." I fill him in on our dinner conversation.

"You like her," Alec observes.

"I do," I acknowledge. "Under different circumstances, I'd want to take my time getting to know her properly."

"But you don't have time," Alec states bluntly.

"Not much, anyway." I rub my face tiredly. "I've been thinking about potential solutions all week. I could find someone willing to marry me just on paper, I suppose."

"What about asking her?" Alec suggests casually.

I stare at him. "Asking Patty to marry me? After one date? That's insane."

"So, take her on another date, then. You have three months. Use them," Alec says.

"That's crazy," I argue. "If we did work out, she'd think I was dating her just to save the ranch." I shake my head. "I don't like the idea of lying. Even for a little while."

"Hear me out," Alec says, turning to face me fully. "You're going to have to ask someone, right?"

"Well, yeah, but—"

"And you actually like this woman," he continues. "She's not a stranger off the street."

"I barely know her," I protest.

"But you want to know her better," Alec points out. "And from what you've said, she seems like someone who might appreciate honesty and partnership over traditional romantic expectations."

"Maybe," I allow, though part of me wonders if that's just wishful thinking.

"Tell her exactly what's at stake. If she's as genuine as you think, she might appreciate your honesty. No games, no pressure."

I shake my head, trying to dismiss the idea. "It's crazy."

"Crazier than losing your family's legacy?" Alec asks quietly. "Or marrying a complete stranger?"

I don't have a good answer for that.

"Look," Alec continues, "I'm not saying you have to decide tonight. Get to know her a bit more, see if there's potential there. But don't dismiss the idea just because it's not how you'd normally go about asking someone to marry you."

"I need to think," I mutter, standing up. I head inside, my mind churning with conflicting thoughts. In my room, I lie on the bed, staring at the ceiling, replaying my evening with Patty.

There was a connection between us. I wasn't imagining that. She seemed genuinely interested, not just being polite. Could someone like her actually be open to an unconventional arrangement if it meant we could explore our connection without the usual dating pressure?

I shake my head. It's absurd. And yet . . .

The more I think about it, the less crazy it sounds. A temporary arrangement, with clear terms. We'd both benefit, and if we get along well, who knows what might develop naturally over time?

Still torn, I think about what Uncle Harry said about selling to another family if I can't meet his requirements. The thought of strangers living in the house where I spent my summers—of someone else's children playing in the orchards—makes my chest tight. This place is more than just land. It's home.

I think of Uncle Harry's decades of work, my grandparents' vision when they started the orchard. I think of the pond where I learned to swim, the barn where I helped deliver my first foal, the orchard rows where we played hide and seek as kids.

And suddenly, the decision doesn't seem so difficult.

I'll see Patty again. Get to know her better. And if our connection deepens like I hope it will, I'll be honest about my situation. If she's the right person, she might understand that sometimes life doesn't follow traditional timelines.

Decision made, I finally drift off to sleep, dreaming of apple blossoms and a woman with a shy smile who might just hold the key to saving everything I love.

CHAPTER FIVE

Patty

I 'm curled up on my couch Saturday evening, reading a book I borrowed from the library, when my phone buzzes with a text message.

Finn: Had a great time last night. Would love to see you again soon. Maybe I could show you the ranch this weekend?

My heart does a little flip. The timing of his message feels almost like he sensed I was thinking about him, because I have been. All day, actually. Our dinner last night keeps replaying in my mind. He was so polite, pulling out my chair, really listening when I talked, the respect in his eyes. So different from what I'm used to.

I felt more comfortable with Finn than I had expected. Safe enough to kiss his cheek goodnight, which was a bold move for me.

I hesitate, my thumbs hovering over the screen. Every instinct honed by years with Klive warns me to be careful, to keep my distance, to protect myself. But another voice—one that sounds suspiciously like

Ms. Daisy—reminds me that not every man is Klive, and hiding forever isn't really living.

Me: I'd like that. I'm off Sunday.

His response comes almost immediately.

Finn: Perfect. I'll pick you up at 11? We could have lunch at the ranch.

Again, I hesitate. Letting someone know where I live, especially a man I've only recently met, goes against all my careful rules. But Finn hasn't given me a reason to not trust him, and the ranch is apparently his family's property, not some isolated location where I'd be vulnerable. Plus, he doesn't *have* to come to my house . . .

Me: That works. Pick me up at the diner?

I hit send and take a breath. Finn is not Klive. He's a good man. I can trust myself.

Finn: Sounds good. See you Sunday at 11.

His message makes me smile. I didn't realize men used emojis. It's cute.

Me: Looking forward to it.

Finn: Sweet dreams, Patty.

As I set my phone down, I find myself wondering what it would be like to have someone like Finn in my corner. Someone who might actually care what happens to me. It's a dangerous train of thought, but as I drift toward sleep, I can't help but imagine a life where I don't have to face every challenge alone.

Sunday morning finds me standing in front of my closet, trying to decide what to wear to a ranch. I've changed clothes three times already, settling on dark jeans and a soft blue sweater that Anne says brings out my eyes. Not that I'm trying to impress anyone.

Who am I kidding? Of course I want Finn to like what he sees.

The thought makes me pause, hairbrush halfway to my head. When did I start caring so much about what he thinks? We've only been on one date, but he's been kind and genuine, and it makes me want to let my guard down in ways that should terrify me.

I arrive at Beats and Eats fifteen minutes early, unable to sit still in my apartment any longer. Ms. Daisy waves from behind the counter where she's restocking coffee cups.

"Well, don't you look pretty," she says with an approving smile. "Off to see that ranch?"

"Just a tour," I say, trying to downplay the flutter of excitement in my chest.

"Mm-hmm." Ms. Daisy's knowing look makes heat creep up my neck. "Have fun, honey. The Millers are good people."

Finn arrives exactly at eleven, and my heart does that little skip it's been doing whenever I see him. He's wearing jeans and a forest green button-down that makes his eyes look even more striking than usual.

"Ready for the grand tour?" he asks, opening the passenger door of his truck for me.

"Absolutely." I slide into the seat, breathing in the faint scent of his cologne mixed with something earthy and clean.

The drive to Apple Blossom Ranch takes us through rolling hills dotted with farms and pastures. Finn points out landmarks as we go, his voice warm with the kind of affection that comes from deep roots.

"That's the Johnson place," he says, nodding toward a red barn. "Their daughter is my age. And see that creek? My brothers and I used to catch crawfish there every summer."

I love listening to him talk about his childhood, the easy way memories flow from him. It's so different from my own past, which I guard like a collection of sharp edges.

"Where'd you grow up?" he asks, glancing over at me.

"Tennessee originally. Small town called Dixie Pass." I keep my voice light, not wanting to delve into why I left. "Not much different from this, really. Everybody knows everybody."

"Do you miss it?"

The question catches me off guard. Do I miss Dixie Pass? The place where Klive systematically cut me off from friends and family until I had no one left but him?

"Sometimes," I say. "I miss the idea of it, anyway. That sense of belonging somewhere."

Finn's expression softens. "And you don't feel that here yet?"

"I'm starting to," I admit. "Piney Brook's been good to me. The people are kind."

"Good," he says simply, but his tone makes me think he genuinely cares about my answer.

We turn down a gravel drive marked by a weathered wooden sign: "Apple Blossom Ranch - Est. 1952." The farmhouse comes into view first, a two-story white building with a wraparound porch and green shutters. It looks like a picture from a magazine about country living, all warm and welcoming.

"It's beautiful," I breathe, taking in the neat flower beds and the swing hanging from the porch ceiling.

"Wait until you see the orchard," Finn says, parking near the house.

A woman emerges from the house as we get out of the truck. She's probably in her sixties, with silver-streaked hair and laugh lines around her eyes. Her smile is immediate and genuine as she approaches us.

"You must be Patty," she says, extending her hand. "I'm Margaret. We've heard so much about you."

I shoot a look at Finn, who has the grace to look slightly embarrassed. "All good things, I hope."

"Oh, yes," Margaret says with a wink. "Finn's quite taken with you."

"Aunt Maggie," Finn warns, but he's smiling.

"What? I'm just being honest." She turns back to me. "Would you like some coffee before your tour? I just put on a fresh pot."

"That sounds wonderful," I say, already charmed by her warmth.

The kitchen is the heart of the house, clearly. It's spacious but cozy, with worn wooden counters and copper pots hanging from hooks. Family photos cover the refrigerator, and the whole space smells like cinnamon and coffee.

Margaret pours three mugs and sets out a plate of what look like homemade oatmeal cookies. "Harry's out checking on the horses," she explains. "You'll get to meet him later."

"Uncle Harry's 'in charge' of the ranch, but Margaret's the real boss around here," Finn says, snagging a cookie.

"Decades of knowing Harry Miller teaches you a thing or two about managing stubborn men," Margaret says with a laugh. "Though I have a feeling Patty might already know about that."

There's nothing pointed in her comment, but I tense slightly anyway. Margaret seems to notice because she smoothly changes the subject.

"Finn tells me you're a gardener. You'll have to see what I've done with the garden behind the house."

"I'd love that," I say, relaxing again. "I've been trying to grow some things in containers, but it's not the same as having actual garden space."

"Container gardening has its challenges," Margaret agrees. "But there's something to be said for being able to move your plants around, find the perfect spot for each one. I usually do a few in pots so I can overwinter them in the greenhouse."

We chat easily about gardening techniques and favorite herbs while we drink our coffee. Margaret has a way of asking questions that feel like genuine interest rather than prying, and I find myself sharing more than I usually would with someone I've just met.

"Ready for that tour?" Finn asks when we've finished our coffee.

"Absolutely."

We start with the garden behind the house, which is exactly the kind of space I've always dreamed of having. Neat rows of rosemary, thyme, and sage . . . and many others, with a small greenhouse tucked into one corner.

"This is incredible," I say, running my fingers over a sprig of lavender.

"Feel free to take some home with you," Margaret offers. "I always have more than I can use."

From there, Finn leads me toward the orchard, and I understand immediately why he's so passionate about this place. The apple trees stretch out in neat rows, their branches heavy with fruit that's almost ready for harvest.

"How many trees?" I ask, trying to take it all in.

"About two hundred producing trees," Finn says, his voice filled with pride. "Some of these were planted by my great-grandfather. The oldest section dates back to the fifties when the ranch was first established."

We walk between the rows, and Finn points out different varieties, explaining the challenges and rewards of each type. His knowledge is impressive, but it's the way his whole face lights up when he talks about the orchard that really captures my attention.

"You really love this," I observe.

"I do," he says simply. "I know it sounds cheesy, but this land is part of me. My family's legacy is literally rooted here."

"It doesn't sound cheesy at all." I stop walking and turn to face him. "It sounds like you know exactly where you belong."

My tone must give me away because Finn's expression grows more serious. "What about you, Patty? Where do you feel like you belong?"

The question hits deeper than I expected. For so long, the answer would have been nowhere. Klive made sure of that, systematically cutting me off from every connection I had until I felt completely lost.

"I'm still figuring that out," I say honestly.

"Maybe it's not about the place," Finn says quietly. "Maybe it's about the people."

I glance up at him, and for a moment, the world narrows to just us. The rustle of the leaves, the distant buzz of bees, the crisp scent of apples—it all fades.

His eyes search mine, soft and steady, like he's waiting for permission.

The space between us feels charged. My heart picks up. I feel an undeniable pull towards him. A part of me wants to close the distance.

But I can't. Not yet.

I take a step back. Just enough to breathe.

Finn doesn't move. Doesn't push.

I clear my throat, forcing a lighter tone. "So," I say, gesturing toward the trees, "what's the secret to picking the perfect apple?"

He lets the moment shift without protest, but his smile remains gentle.

"It's all about the weight," he says. "A ripe one feels just right in your hand. Solid, but not too heavy. But if you're looking for a pitching apple . . ."

"What's a pitching apple?" I ask as Finn bends down and reaches into the grass at the base of the tree.

He pulls up a brown, mushy castoff and says, "This," chucking the rotten apple at the trunk of a nearby tree.

It explodes into a spray of applesauce, and I jump, causing us both to laugh.

We spend the rest of the afternoon exploring the ranch. Finn shows me the barn where they store equipment, the small pasture where they keep a few cattle, and the creek that runs along the back of the property. Everything he shows me comes with stories about his childhood, his brothers, the summers they spent here working alongside their uncle.

"That one?" he says, nodding toward Clarabelle, who's currently eyeing us with regal disapproval from under a tree. "She thinks she owns the place. Alec calls her Duchess Clarabelle Mooington."

I laugh. "She looks like she believes it."

"She does," he says dryly. "And heaven help us if someone forgets to latch a gate."

"She's feisty, then?" I ask, chuckling as she lets out an indignant moo.

"That's one way of putting it," Finn says, shaking his head. "She's a trouble maker."

We walk along a path, our hands brushing occasionally until we reach the creek.

"You were lucky to have this place growing up," I say as we sit on a fallen log beside the babbling water.

"I was," he agrees. "Though I didn't always appreciate it at the time. When you're fifteen, spending your summer working the ranch doesn't feel nearly as exciting as it does now."

"And now you're taking it over?"

"That's the plan." His expression grows more serious. "Uncle Harry's ready to retire, and someone needs to keep the family legacy going. I want it to be me."

"He's lucky to have you."

"I hope so." Finn picks up a smooth stone and skips it across the water. "Sometimes I wonder if I'm crazy for taking on so much responsibility. Most guys my age are focused on advancing their careers and making big money, not worrying about apple harvests and livestock."

"Do you want to be most guys your age?"

He considers this. "No. I want to be the kind of man who builds something lasting. Who contributes to his community instead of just taking from it."

The conviction in his voice makes a warm feeling unfurl in my chest. This is a man who knows his values, who isn't afraid of hard work or commitment.

"That's admirable," I say.

"What about you?" he asks. "What do you want to build?"

The question catches me off guard. For so long, my goals have been purely about survival, getting away from Klive, finding safety, and making it through each day. The idea of building a relationship, of looking toward a future instead of just escaping the past, feels both strange and appealing.

"I want to feel settled somewhere," I say finally. "I want to wake up in the morning and not wonder if I'll have to run again."

Finn's brow furrows. "Run from what?"

I realize too late how much I've revealed. "Just . . . changes, I guess. Moving around gets old."

He studies my face like he's trying to read between the lines, but he doesn't push. "Well, Piney Brook's a good place to put down roots. People here take care of each other."

"So I'm learning."

As the sun starts to set, we make our way back to the house. Margaret has dinner waiting. Pot roast with vegetables and fresh bread that makes my mouth water just looking at it.

Harry Miller turns out to be exactly what I expected from Ms. Daisy's description. A sturdy man in his sixties with calloused hands and kind eyes greets me with the same warmth Margaret showed. He asks thoughtful questions about my work at the diner and my impressions of Piney Brook.

"This one treating you right?" Harry asks, nodding toward Finn.

"He's been a perfect gentleman," I assure him.

"Good. He wasn't raised to be anything less."

Dinner conversation flows easily, touching on everything from local politics to the upcoming apple festival. Margaret insists I take home a container of leftovers and a bundle of herbs from her garden.

"You'll have to come back soon," she says as Finn and I prepare to leave. "Maybe for Sunday dinner sometime?"

The invitation catches me off guard. I'm not used to being included in family gatherings, especially by people I've just met.

"I'd like that," I say, meaning it more than I expected to.

On the drive back to town, Finn and I are quiet, both lost in our own thoughts. The evening feels significant, like our relationship has shifted. All I can think about is how safe Finn makes me feel.

"Thank you for today," I say as he walks me to my car parked next to Beats and Eats. "Your family is wonderful."

"They liked you too," he says. "I could tell. My brothers wanted to be here, but work called. Trust me, you'd never have survived the stories."

We stand there for a moment, the air between us charged with possibility. I rise up on my toes and kiss his cheek, letting my lips linger just a moment longer than necessary.

"Can I follow you home? Just to make sure you get there safely?" he asks me. "I'd like to see you again, if you're up for it."

"Okay," I tell him, deciding to take a chance.

When we get to my apartment, Finn pulls up beside the walkway and rolls his window down.

"Goodnight, Finn."

"Goodnight, Patty."

Looking out, I see he's still idling there. Waving, I watch from my window as he drives away, my heart full of feelings I'm almost afraid to name. For the first time in longer than I can remember, I'm excited about the future instead of just trying to survive it.

CHAPTER SIX

Finn

I'm up before dawn again, my mind already on the day ahead. The harvest season is approaching fast, and there's still so much to coordinate. But even as I review the crew schedules and equipment lists spread across the kitchen table, my thoughts keep drifting to Patty.

It's been three days since our ranch tour, and I can't stop thinking about how she looked standing in that orchard, touching the bark of my grandfather's trees with such reverence. Or how her face lit up when I showed her the garden. Her laughter when I threw the bad apple and it exploded. Being with her makes everything seem more vibrant.

My phone buzzes with a text.

Patty: *Thank you again for Sunday. I keep thinking about that pond.*

I smile, typing back immediately.

Me: *It's one of my favorite spots. Maybe we could go back there soon?*

Patty: *I'd like that.*

Before I can second-guess myself, I add another message.

Me: *Are you free tonight? I could cook dinner at the cottage, show you more of the property.*

Her response takes a few minutes, long enough that I start to worry I'm pushing too hard.

Patty: *That sounds wonderful. What time?*

Me: *Six? I'll pick you up at your place.*

Patty: *Perfect.*

I'm grinning like an idiot when Uncle Harry walks into the kitchen, already dressed for the day.

"You're looking mighty pleased with yourself this morning," he observes, pouring coffee.

"Just making plans," I say, trying to play it casual.

Uncle Harry raises an eyebrow. "Plans involving a certain young lady from the diner?"

There's no point denying it. "I'm cooking dinner for Patty tonight. At the cottage."

"Ah," Uncle Harry nods approvingly. "Good. Take your time getting to know her properly."

"What do you mean?"

He settles across from me at the table. "I mean don't let this inheritance deadline rush you into anything you're not ready for. If she's the right woman, she'll still be the right woman whether you marry her in three months or three years."

"I appreciate that," I say carefully. "But you're the one who set the timeline."

Uncle Harry's expression grows more serious. "I know what I said, Finn. But I'd rather sell the ranch than see you rush into a relationship that isn't right."

His words stick with me as I head out to check on the orchard. The apple trees are heavy with fruit that's almost ready for picking. In another week, we'll have crews here around the clock, the peaceful quiet of the ranch replaced with the organized chaos of harvest season.

I'm inspecting the irrigation system when my phone rings. Cooper's name flashes on the screen.

"Hey, brother," I answer. "What's going on?"

"That's what I want to know," Cooper says. "Caleb and I were just talking, and we realized we haven't heard from you since the wedding. Usually you'd call to complain by this time."

I laugh. "Maybe I don't have anything to complain about."

"Or maybe you're distracted," Caleb's voice chimes in. They must have me on speaker. "Word is you've been spending a lot of time in town lately."

"And where exactly are you hearing this?"

"Alec mentioned you've been to the diner several times this week," Cooper says. "Plus, I'm still missing my good cologne."

"Smells better on me anyway," I tease.

"So it's true!" Caleb sounds delighted. "You're dating the waitress. Tell us about her."

I pause, considering how much to share. "Her name's Patty," I remind them.

"The waitress who was flirting with you, right?" Cooper asks.

"She wasn't flirting—"

"Well, she sure wasn't backing down from the attention," Caleb interrupts. "Speaking of which, I still want to know where that came from. You've never been smooth with women."

"Thanks for the confidence boost," I say dryly.

"So what's she like?" Cooper asks. "Besides pretty."

I find myself smiling. "She's kind. Smart. Strong, though I don't think she realizes it. There's something about her that just feels . . . right."

There's a pause on the other end of the line.

"Whoa," Cooper says. "You're falling for her."

"This is huge," Caleb says. "Our confirmed bachelor brother is actually smitten."

"I am not smitten," I protest, though the denial sounds weak even to me.

"You are so smitten," Cooper laughs. "I can hear it in your voice. You get all soft when you talk about her."

"I do not get soft."

"You absolutely do," Caleb confirms. "So when are you seeing her again?"

"Tonight, actually. I'm cooking dinner for her."

"Look at you, Mr. Romance," Caleb teases. "What are you making?"

"I was thinking of grilling some steaks, making a salad. Nothing too fancy."

"Good choice," Cooper approves. "Keep it simple. And Finn?"

"Yeah?"

"Don't overthink it. Just be yourself."

"I'm not sure being myself will help." Taking a deep breath, I decide to confide in them about the things Patty has shared with me. "I get the feeling that her ex, Klive, was a real piece of work."

After I hang up, I spend the rest of the morning coordinating with Alec about the harvest schedule. The crews will start arriving on Monday, and we want everything ready to go.

"You seem distracted today," Alec observes as we check the equipment in the main barn.

"Just a lot on my mind," I tell him. "Making sure we're ready for harvest."

"Uh-huh." He doesn't look convinced. "And a certain brunette?"

I sigh. "Does everyone need to comment on my personal life today?"

"Just looking out for you," Alec grins. "She seemed nice when we met her. Sweet. Like *sugar*."

He laughs at his joke, and I roll my eyes, though I can't help but smile.

"By the way, Clarabelle was out again this morning. Found her munching on grass near the horse barn when I went to check on Gus and Buttercup."

I groan. "Did she give you any trouble getting her back to the field?"

"Nah, just the usual. You know she's a sucker for sweet tea. I bribed her." Alec laughs. "I know you don't like her, but she's got too much personality to let go."

"It's not that I don't like her. She's just trouble with a capital T."

That afternoon, I drive into town to pick up groceries for dinner. I want everything to be perfect. At the grocery store, I pick out two beautiful ribeye steaks, grab fresh vegetables for a salad and some tomatoes.

On impulse, I stop by the florist and buy a small bouquet of sunflowers. They remind me of Patty—bright and cheerful, but strong, too.

By five-thirty, I'm at the cottage, steaks marinating and salad prepared. I've set the small table on the front porch, where we can watch the sunset over the orchard. The sunflowers sit in a mason jar in the center, simple but welcoming.

When I pull up to Ruth's house at six, Patty's waiting on the front steps. She's changed out of her work clothes into a light yellow dress that brings out the gold highlights in her hair. She looks beautiful.

"Hi," she says as I approach. "You look nice."

"Thanks," I reply. It's great she noticed my clean blue button-down—it's the third one I tried on.

"I brought dessert." She picks up a covered dish from a little side table. "Apple crisp. I thought it seemed appropriate."

"Perfect," I say, meaning it. The thoughtfulness of bringing a dish made specifically for tonight impresses me—*she* impresses me over and over. I carry the dish to the truck for her, and when I help her into her seat, I feel like I don't want to let go of her hand.

At the cottage, I give her the tour, showing her the cozy space where seasonal workers sometimes stay. The stone cottage has a nice big fireplace and a great view of the orchard. She calls it "charming" and it makes me want to hand her a deed to it before dessert.

We move to the porch where I start the grill. Patty settles into one of the wooden chairs, watching as I tend to the steaks.

"Tell me about harvest season," she says. "What's it like?"

"Organized chaos," I admit with a laugh. "We'll have crews picking from dawn to dusk. The goal is to get everything harvested at peak ripeness, processed, and either shipped fresh or stored properly for later sales."

"How many people?"

"About twenty seasonal workers, plus our regular crew of three. They stay in the bunkhouse, and Margaret coordinates meals for everyone."

"That's a lot of mouths to feed," she observes.

"Maggie's a miracle worker," I agree. "She's kept things in line as the cook and housekeeper of the ranch as long as I can remember. Though she's been talking about wanting help this year. She's not as young as she used to be."

Patty looks thoughtful. "That sounds challenging. I bet the crew becomes like family during harvest."

"They do," I confirm. "It's one of my favorite things about this time of year. Everyone working together toward a common goal."

The steaks are perfect, and we eat as the sun sets over the orchard, painting the sky in brilliant oranges and pinks. Patty tells me more about her grandmother, who taught her to cook and garden. I share stories about learning to work the ranch from my grandfather, the lessons that shaped who I am today.

"It must be nice," she says wistfully, "having such deep roots here."

"You could have that too," I tell her. "Roots, I mean. If you wanted them."

There was vulnerability in her eyes as she looked at me. "I'd like that. More than I probably should."

"Why shouldn't you?"

"Because I've learned not to count on things lasting," she says quietly. "People leave, or they change, or situations fall apart. It's safer not to get too attached."

The sadness in her voice makes me want to promise her that not everything has to end, that some things are worth holding on to. But we're not there yet, so instead I reach across the table and take her hand.

"Some things last," I say simply. "This ranch has been in my family for three generations. These trees have been producing fruit for sixty years. Good things don't always go away, Patty."

She squeezes my hand, her eyes bright with emotion. "I'm starting to believe that might be true."

I grin. "Good. Because otherwise I'm just a guy dragging you through a bunch of trees for no reason."

She lets out a soft laugh. "You mean this isn't part of some elaborate orchard cult initiation?"

"Not unless it involves pie," I say. "And maybe cider. Definitely flannel."

Her laughter bubbles out again, light and free, and I want to make her laugh like that again and again.

After dinner, we walk through the orchard as twilight settles around us. The air is crisp with the promise of autumn, and the scent of ripening apples fills the evening breeze.

"When will you start picking?" she asks, reaching up to touch a particularly heavy cluster of fruit.

"Monday," I tell her. "The Galas are ready first, then the Honeycrisps, then the Fujis. Each variety has its perfect moment."

"How do you know when they're ready?"

I select an apple from a nearby branch and hand it to her. "Try it."

She takes a bite, juice running down her chin. Her eyes widen at the sweetness. "Oh my goodness, that's incredible."

"That's how you know," I say, reaching up to brush the juice from her chin with my thumb. "Perfect flavor, perfect texture. That's a Gala at its peak."

The moment stretches between us, my hand still resting against her cheek, her eyes locked on mine. I want to kiss her so badly it's almost painful, but a feeling holds me back. The knowledge that she's been hurt, that she needs to feel safe before she can trust completely.

Instead, I let my hand fall away, though I don't step back.

"We should head back," she says, her voice slightly breathless. "I have an early shift tomorrow."

"Of course," I agree, though I'm reluctant to end the evening.

The drive back to town is quiet. I wish she would confide in me about whatever put those shadows in her eyes. When I walk her to her door, she turns to face me, her hand on the doorknob.

"Thank you for tonight," she says. "Dinner was wonderful. The cottage is beautiful."

"Thank you for coming," I reply. "For giving me a chance to show you more of the ranch."

She steps closer, rising on her toes to press a soft kiss to my cheek. It's brief, innocent, but it sends warmth spreading through my entire body.

"Goodnight, Finn," she whispers.

"Goodnight, Patty," I manage.

I wait until she's safely inside before returning to my truck, and I put my hand over the kiss spot that's still tingling.

As I drive back to the ranch, I think about my brothers' words. They're right—I am falling for her. Hard. The question is whether she's falling too.

The sweet way she looked at me tonight, her soft kiss on my cheek. . . it felt like the beginning of something real.

I just hope I'm reading the signs correctly, because somewhere between that first day at the diner and tonight, Patty Walsh has become a lot more than just a potential solution to Uncle Harry's requirements.

She's become the woman I can't stop thinking about, can't imagine not having in my life.

And that realization unsettles me because I'm starting to think there's nothing I wouldn't give to keep her by my side. Including the ranch.

CHAPTER SEVEN

Patty

The lunch rush winds down and I'm wiping the counter when my mind drifts back to yesterday. The sweet smell of ripe apples, Finn's steady hand as we walked the orchard, that he let me step away from the moment instead of pushing.

He's unlike anyone I've known. I'm still smiling when my phone buzzes.

Finn: *Any interest in ice skating tomorrow afternoon?*

My stomach does a little flip. Ice skating sounds terrifying and wonderful all at once.

"What's got you smiling like that?" Anne asks, sliding onto a counter stool. She must have just finished with a client at the salon.

I show her the text, and her eyes light up. "Ice skating! That's so romantic. Say yes!"

"I've never been," I admit, hesitating.

"Even better," Anne grins. "He can teach you, hold your hand the whole time . . ."

The image makes my stomach flutter. "What if I fall on my face?"

"Then he helps you up," Ms. Daisy chimes in from behind the counter. "That's what good men do, honey."

Taking a deep breath, I type my reply.

Me: *I'd love to, but fair warning, I've never skated before.*

His response comes quickly.

Finn: *Perfect opportunity to learn. I'll be gentle, promise. Meet at the rink at 7?*

Me: *Yes. Looking forward to it.*

"You're glowing," Anne observes with satisfaction. "I haven't seen you this happy since . . . Actually, I don't think I've ever seen you this happy."

She's right. Despite my nerves about skating, I'm excited to see Finn again. Last night's dinner at the cottage was perfect. How he looked at me in the orchard when we were talking about the apple harvest, like I was precious . . . it made me feel things I'd thought were lost forever.

"He makes me feel safe," I admit quietly. "Like I can just be myself."

Ms. Daisy's expression softens. "That's how you know he's a keeper, honey."

The next evening I'm sitting on a bench at the indoor ice rink, lacing up rental skates with trembling fingers. The rink is large and filled with people who all seem to know what they're doing. My eye catches on a young woman spinning graceful circles on what I'm mentally calling "death blades." It's magical, but would be even more so if I weren't absolutely certain I'm about to injure myself.

"Need help with those?"

I look up to find Finn standing before me, already wearing his skates. He's bundled in a navy jacket that makes his eyes look striking, and his smile sends warmth through me that I'm sure is melting the ice inside the rink.

"I think I've got it," I say, pulling the laces tight. "Though I can't promise the same for the actual skating part."

Finn laughs, the sound rich and warm. "Everyone falls their first time. The trick is learning how to fall gracefully."

"Is there such a thing?"

"Not really," he admits with that honest charm I'm growing to love, extending his hand to help me up. "But it sounds better than saying 'try not to land on your face.'"

His honesty coaxes a laugh from me as I wobble to my feet, clinging to his arm for balance. The skates feel strange and wobbly, and we're not even on the ice yet.

"Ready?" he asks.

"As I'll ever be."

Finn guides me to the rink entrance, one arm wrapped securely around my waist. "Small steps at first," he instructs. "And remember to breathe."

The moment my blades touch the ice, I tense, certain I'm about to fall. But Finn's arm remains steady around me, his other hand holding mine.

"I've got you," he murmurs, close to my ear. "Trust me."

And I do. After last night, trust feels less scary than it used to. Little by little, he teaches me to glide, to shift my weight from one foot to the other. We move slowly along the edge of the rink, other skaters flowing gracefully past us.

"You're a natural," Finn says after I manage a few pushes without clutching his arm in terror.

"You're a liar," I laugh, "but a kind one."

Eventually, I grow brave enough to try skating while holding just his hand instead of his entire arm. We move in sync, and I forget to be afraid. We're comfortable together, and I'm starting to believe maybe it's okay to let go and enjoy the moment.

Until my skate catches on the ice and suddenly I'm falling. Finn tries to catch me, but momentum pulls us both down. We land in a tangle of limbs, me on top of him, his arms wrapped protectively around me.

"Are you okay?" we ask simultaneously, then break into laughter.

I manage to get halfway off him before his foot slips out from under him again and we both go down—again—narrowly avoiding taking out a little kid.

"Okay," he says, flat on his back. "New plan. We live here now."

I laugh. "We can become penguins," I say, pushing to my feet, carefully.

Once we're both standing, Finn leads me to the wall. "Seriously, are you okay? Nothing's hurt?"

"I think my dignity is bruised," I say, trying to stay upright without grabbing the wall, or him.

"Dignity heals," he replies, grinning as I flail my arms in an attempt to stay standing. "Besides, I promised we'd both end up on the ice at some point."

"Ah, so that was your fault," I say to him, grinning and raising my eyebrows at him.

He smiles and shakes his head at me. "Yes, I ordered the extra slippery ice for today," he says and pulls me away from the wall.

We skate for another hour, until my ankles ache and my cheeks hurt from smiling. Finn never lets go of my hand, not even when I gain enough confidence to move a bit faster. By the end, I'm not exactly graceful, but I'm upright and moving under my own power.

After turning in our skates, Finn suggests hot chocolate from the concessions booth. We find a quiet bench and sip our warm drinks, our breath fogging in the cool air.

"Thank you," I say, warming my hands on the cup. "This was really fun. Even if I did take us both down."

Finn grins. "Worth it. Besides, it gave me an excuse to hold your hand all evening."

My cheeks warm, and not from the hot chocolate. "Smooth talker."

"Only when I mean it." His eyes hold mine, and there's no teasing in them now, only a sincerity that makes my heart skip.

We sit in silence for a while, watching other skaters circle the rink. Finn's shoulder presses against mine, warm and solid. I think about how different this feels from anything I experienced with Klive. There's no pressure here, no sense that I need to be anyone other than who I am.

After a while, Finn turns to me. "Harvest starts Monday. It's going to be crazy around the ranch for the next few weeks. But I'd still like to see you, if you're up for it."

I blink, surprised. "You'd want me around during that kind of chaos?"

He nods. "Absolutely. Even just for lunch or a short visit. In case you haven't noticed, I enjoy your company."

"I'm off Sundays, and sometimes I can get a Wednesday afternoon if it's slow."

Finn's whole face lights up. "Perfect. Come by any time. I'll provide the snacks." He winks. "Hope you like apples."

I laugh. "You're in luck. They happen to be my favorite fruit."

As we walk to our cars, our hands find each other naturally. At my car, Finn turns to face me, a small smile tugging at his lips.

"Patty," he says, softly. "You're easy to be around. I really enjoy this." He motions between the two of us with his free hand. "Being with you."

The simple words mean more than any flowery declaration could. "I like being with you, too, Finn."

He smiles, then leans down to press a gentle kiss to my cheek. It's soft and only lasts a second, but it sends warmth spreading through my entire body.

"Sweet dreams," he murmurs.

"You too," I whisper back.

As I drive home, I can't stop smiling. Tomorrow starts harvest season, and it sounds like I've landed myself right in the middle of it all. More importantly, I've found myself falling for a man who makes me feel like I deserve a wonderful life.

For the first time in years, I'm not bracing for impact.

I'm leaning forward, toward something good.

That hope is scary, but it's the sweetest part of all.

CHAPTER EIGHT

Finn

The ladder shifts slightly under my boots as I reach for another cluster of apples. Harvest day one, and the crew's been at it for two hours. Sunlight filters through the trees, dappling the rows where workers move with the practiced rhythm of experience. The sound of voices and rustling branches fills the morning air, punctuated by the occasional thud of apples hitting canvas bags.

I twist the nearest apple with the motion Uncle Harry taught me when I was twelve. . . lift, twist, release. The fruit comes away clean, stem intact, perfect for storage. Some things never change, even when the world feels like it's spinning out of control.

"Finn!" Alec calls from a few trees down, waving a grease-stained hand. "We've got a belt problem at the sorting station."

Perfect. "I'll take a look."

I climb down carefully, my shoulders already tight from the morning's work. The sorting station is the heart of our operation. If it's not running smoothly, we'll have apples backing up faster than we can handle them. Just past the orchard, I spot Margaret heading our way with a thermos and what looks like a tin of biscuits.

The sight of her reminds me of the deadline I've been trying not to think about all morning. It's been a couple of weeks since that conversation in the kitchen, and I'm no closer to being married than I was then. Well, that's not entirely true. I'm closer to wanting to be married. To Patty specifically. But I don't dare bring it up to her yet.

"Coffee break!" Margaret calls cheerfully, and the crew starts drifting toward the picnic tables under the oak tree.

Uncle Harry emerges from the direction of the barn, hands on his hips, surveying the morning's progress with the critical eye of a man who's overseen forty harvest seasons. His weathered face shows satisfaction at what he sees, but I catch the way his gaze lingers on me.

"How's the yield?" he asks as I approach.

"Better than I expected," I say, accepting a steaming cup from Margaret. The coffee's strong and black, exactly what I need. "If the machines hold up, we might get ahead this week."

He nods, then gives me a sidelong glance that I've been dreading. "And how are things going with that girl of yours?"

Right to it, then. I should have known he wouldn't let me avoid this conversation forever.

"They're good," I say cautiously. "Better than good."

"But . . . ?"

I take a sip of coffee, buying time. Around us, the crew settles into easy conversation, the kind of comfortable chatter that comes when people have worked together before. Miguel, our crew leader, is already planning the afternoon's rotation. Sarah, one of our newer workers, asks

Margaret about the best places to eat in town. Normal harvest day talk. Nothing about forced nuptials or life-changing decisions.

"*But* I haven't told her about the marriage stipulation."

Uncle Harry's face doesn't change, but disappointment fills his eyes. "It's been a few weeks already, Finn."

"I know." The words come out heavier than I intended. "I just ... she's been through a lot. I'm not going to rush her. And if I tell her now, it'll sound like I've had an ulterior motive this whole time."

"Have you?"

The question is like a punch to the gut. When Uncle Harry first laid out the terms, I didn't know what to think, except that I needed time. Patty had already caught my eye. From the first day we met, things about her stuck with me. How she listened and responded to me. But then she carried herself like she was trying not to take up too much space.

"No," I say, without hesitation. "This thing with Patty started before I ever knew about the clause. And now, I'm in it for her. I care about her."

Uncle Harry's expression softens. "Care about her how?"

I look out over the orchard, watching the crew work. These trees have been producing fruit since before I was born. Some of them were planted by my great-grandfather's hands. Being here, surrounded by this legacy, makes truth feel unavoidable.

"I think I'm falling in love with her," I admit quietly.

"You think?"

"I know." The admission feels like stepping off a cliff. "When I think about the future, about running this place, I can't picture it without her."

Uncle Harry's quiet for a long moment, studying my face. "Then you owe her honesty," he says gently. "The ranch is just land, son. That girl's one of a kind."

Before I can respond, Alec jogs up with a grease-smeared wrench in his hand. "We got it running again. For now. Might need to replace the pulley next week."

"Good work," I tell him, grateful for the interruption. "Let's get back to it."

The rest of the morning passes in a blur of ladders, sweat, and full apple bins. With every apple dropped into the bin, my thoughts settle. Harvest has a way of pulling you into the moment and grounding you in what matters. My family's done this for generations, but today feels more personal than ever.

By lunch, we've made real progress. The Honeycrisps are coming off clean and sweet, and the early yield estimates are looking optimistic. As the crew settles under the oak tree for sandwiches and sweet tea, I find myself beside Alec, staring into the distance.

"You're quiet," he observes, unwrapping a turkey sandwich.

"Thinking."

"About her?"

I glance over. Alec's worked here for most of his life. He's been around long enough to read the rhythms of the ranch and the people on it. He's maybe five years younger than me, with the kind of easy confidence that comes from knowing exactly what you want out of life.

"Yeah."

Alec doesn't push. Just nods, like he gets it. "She seems nice."

"She is."

"Good for you, then." He takes another bite of sandwich. "You've been different lately. Happier."

Have I? I suppose I have been. Even with Uncle Harry's deadline hanging over my head, and the weight of the ranch's future pressing down on me, thinking about Patty makes everything lighter.

"Thanks," I say, not sure what else to add.

"Whatever you're working through," Alec says, "remember that good women don't come along every day. When you find one, you better hold on."

His words stick with me as we finish lunch and head back to work. The afternoon sun is merciless, beating down on us as we move through the rows. My shirt's soaked with sweat, and my hands are sticky with apple juice, but there's satisfaction in the work. Physical labor has a way of clearing the mind, of making complex problems feel manageable.

But as the sun starts to sink lower, Uncle Harry's words echo in my head. The ranch is just land. It can be replaced. Patty can't.

Back at the house, Margaret calls to me while loading empty trays into the kitchen sink. Her silver hair's pulled back in a bun, and there's flour dusting her apron from the afternoon's baking.

"I could use another set of hands this week," she says without preamble. "Feeding this many people is no joke."

"I'll ask around town," I offer, though my mind's already racing ahead to an obvious solution.

"I was hoping you'd ask Patty."

That makes me pause. Margaret's face doesn't give away her thoughts, but there's a sparkle in her eyes that suggests she knows exactly what she's doing.

"I know she works at the diner," Margaret continues, "but if she has any afternoons off, I'd be grateful for the help. And I think she'd enjoy being part of this."

The idea takes root immediately. Patty, here, helping prep meals, laughing in the kitchen with Margaret, becoming part of the daily rhythm of harvest season. It feels right. More than right. It feels like I've wanted her here, beside me, without realizing it.

"What kind of help do you need?" I ask.

"Meal prep, mostly. Chopping vegetables, helping with bread, serving the crew. Nothing complicated, but it's a lot of work for one person." Margaret pauses, studying my face. "She'd fit right in, I think. She's got that gentle way about her that puts people at ease."

I think about Patty at the diner, how she remembers everyone's regular order, how she makes conversation with the customers without making them feel uncomfortable. Margaret's right. She would fit.

"I'll call her," I say.

Margaret beams. "Wonderful. Tell her I'll teach her everything she needs to know. And Finn—"

"Yeah?"

"She makes you smile more. I like that."

Heat creeps up my neck. "Is it that obvious?"

"To someone who's been watching you boys grow up, yes." Margaret's smile turns softer. "I want you to know that whatever you decide, we support you. But don't let timelines push you into a relationship that isn't right."

"What if it is right, though?" The question slips out before I can stop it.

"Then you'll know," Margaret says simply. "And so will she."

That night, after dinner and the endless chores that come with running a ranch, I step onto the porch with my phone in hand. The sky is clear, stars bright above the orchard. Crickets chirp in the grass, and in the distance, I can hear the low murmur of voices from the bunkhouse where the crew's settling in for the night.

I dial Patty's number before I can talk myself out of it.

"Hey," she answers, and I can hear the smile in her voice. "How was harvest?"

"Hot. Satisfying. Loud. Plus, Clarabelle got out again, so that was interesting. Found her snacking on low-hanging Fujis. I swear, she's got to be related to Houdini himself." I grin, settling into one of the porch chairs. "How was the diner?"

"Slow. Ms. Daisy tried to guess how many times I fell skating."

"Let me guess. She said six?"

"Eight. I told her only twice."

"She believed you?"

"No, but she pretended to."

We both laugh, the kind of easy, warm sound that's starting to feel like home. This is what I love about talking to Patty. It's natural. She makes everything feel lighter, happier.

"I actually called to ask a favor," I say, my heart picking up speed. "Margaret's swamped with meals for the crew. She was wondering if you'd be willing to help out a couple days a week. Prep work, mostly. If you're free."

There's a pause, and I find myself holding my breath.

"You want me to work at the ranch?"

"Only if you want to," I say quickly. "No pressure. I just think you'd enjoy it. And I'd like having you around more."

The honesty of that last part surprises me. But it's true. The thought of seeing Patty more often, of having her be part of this place that means everything to me, fills me with warmth.

Another pause. Longer this time.

"I could probably shift things with Ms. Daisy," she says slowly. "She's been nudging me to take more time off anyway."

I wait, heart ticking like a countdown clock.

"You're sure Margaret wouldn't mind?"

"She asked for you specifically. And she'll train you on everything. The crew's easy to please. They just want good food and plenty of it."

"Okay," she says. "I'll do it."

Relief flows through me like cool water. "Really?"

"Really. It sounds like fun, actually." She takes a breath, letting it out slowly. "Finn?" Her voice softens, becomes more tentative. "You're not just asking because of *us*, are you?"

The question catches me off guard. "No. Not even a little." I swallow, choosing my words carefully. "Margaret really needs help. You're great with people. And . . . I like seeing you here. It feels right."

She doesn't answer right away, but when she does, her voice is warm. "Okay. I'll see you Wednesday."

"I'll pick you up," I offer.

"I can drive myself—"

"Patty." My voice drops. "You don't need me to, I know that. But I'd really like to pick you up. If you'll let me. It'll be a nice break for me, and it will give me a little time to hold your hand."

"Okay," she says softly. "I'll see you Wednesday."

After we hang up, I stay on the porch for a long time, watching the dark outline of the orchard sway in the breeze. Lost in my thoughts.

Patty's coming here. Becoming part of this place, this life I want. The thought fills me with hope. Like it's the beginning of a future I'm finally brave enough to picture.

It's everything I didn't know I needed.

Now I just have to find the courage to tell her the truth about Uncle Harry's deadline, what's at stake, and how I feel before my silence becomes the thing that keeps her away.

The stars sparkle overhead, same as they have for generations of Millers working this land. If you're willing to put in the work, some things do endure.

I just hope what Patty and I are building will be one of them.

My heart races in anticipation. I want to spend more time with her before harvest kicks into high gear.

I pull out my phone and scroll through the local events calendar for Barberville. Cowboy Church's monthly barn dance is this Saturday night. Perfect timing.

Before I can second-guess myself, I type out a message.

Me: *One more thing. There's a barn dance Saturday night at the church in Barberville. Live music, dancing, the whole community comes out. Any interest in letting me teach you how to two-step?*

Her response comes quickly.

Patty: *That sounds terrifying and wonderful. Yes!*

Me: Perfect. Fair warning, I might step on your toes.

Patty: *I'll take my chances.*

I'm grinning like an idiot as I head inside. Saturday can't come fast enough.

CHAPTER NINE

Patty

I check my reflection in the bathroom mirror one more time, smoothing down my hair and adjusting the belt on my favorite sundress. When Finn asked if I'd like to go to the barn dance, I wasn't sure what to expect. But the thrill of spending more time with him made it impossible to say no.

My phone buzzes with a text.

Finn: *On my way. Can't wait to see you.*

The butterflies in my stomach take flight. It's been several weeks since our first date, and every moment with Finn feels like a breath of fresh air. He makes me laugh. He listens when I talk. Most importantly, he makes me feel safe, which I'd forgotten was possible.

I grab my cardigan and purse just as I hear his truck pull up outside. Through the window, I watch him hop out and head toward my apartment, and my heart does a familiar skip. He's wearing dark jeans, a crisp white button-down, and cowboy boots that look like they've seen some actual work, but he's got them shined up tonight.

"Evening, beautiful," he says when I open the door, his eyes lighting up as he takes in my appearance. "You look incredible."

"Thank you." I feel heat rise in my cheeks. "You don't look too bad yourself, cowboy."

"Ready to cut a rug?" he asks, offering me his arm.

"As ready as I'll ever be. Though I should warn you, my dancing experience is limited to swaying awkwardly at high school dances."

Finn laughs, a rich sound that always makes me smile. "Lucky for you, I'm an excellent teacher. Plus, if you step on my toes, I'll just pretend it's part of the dance."

The drive to Barberville takes us through rolling countryside dotted with farmhouses and pastures. Finn points out landmarks along the way—the creek where he and his brothers used to catch crawfish, the old oak tree they climbed every summer, the field where Cooper once got chased by an angry bull.

"Tell me about these barn dances," I say, curious about what I'm walking into. "Are they really in a barn?"

"The church has this beautiful old barn they've converted to use for community events," Finn explains. "Once a month, they clear it out, bring in a local band, and half the county shows up to dance. It's nothing fancy, just good music and good people having fun together."

"Sounds perfect," I say, meaning it.

When we arrive, I can hear the music drifting from the large red barn behind the small white church. Lights are strung between the trees, and couples of all ages are making their way toward the entrance. The parking lot's full of trucks and cars, and everyone seems to know everyone else.

"Nervous?" Finn asks, taking my hand as we walk toward the barn.

"A little," I admit. "What if I make a fool of myself?"

"Then you'll fit right in," he says with a grin. "Half the fun is watching people who don't know what they're doing. It's all about having a good time, not being the best dancer or couple on the floor."

Inside the barn, the scene is exactly what Finn described. The space has been cleared and decorated with lights and hay bales arranged as seating around the edges. A four-piece band plays on a small stage at the far end, and the dance floor is already full of couples spinning and stepping in a way that looks complicated but effortless.

"Finn Miller!" calls a woman's voice. We turn to see a middle-aged woman with graying hair and a warm smile approaching us. "I haven't seen you at one of these in ages."

"Mrs. Richards," Finn says, giving her a quick hug. "Good to see you. This is Patty Walsh. Patty, this is Amelia Richards. She runs the church's community outreach program."

"Wonderful to meet you, dear," Mrs. Richards says, shaking my hand. "Are you new to the area?"

"Relatively," I say. "I work at Beats and Eats in Piney Brook."

"Oh, Ms. Daisy's place! She's a treasure. Well, you picked a good one to bring you tonight," she says, nodding toward Finn. "The Miller boys know how to dance."

Before I can respond, she's spotted someone else she needs to greet and bustles away. Finn chuckles and guides me toward the dance floor.

"Ready for your first lesson?" he asks.

"I guess so. Just promise you won't laugh if I trip over my own feet."

"I would never," he says solemnly, then grins. "Okay, I might laugh a little, but only if it's really funny."

The current song ends, and the band strikes up a song with a steadier beat. Finn positions us at the edge of the dance floor where there's more room for error.

"Two-step is easy once you get the rhythm," he explains, taking my right hand in his left and placing his other hand on my waist. "It's quick-quick-slow-slow. Like this."

He demonstrates the basic step, and I try to follow along. At first, I'm so focused on my feet that I barely notice anything else. But as I start to get the hang of it, I become aware of Finn's hand steady on my back.

"You're getting it," he says, as we make our way around the floor. "Just relax and let me lead."

Relaxing doesn't come naturally to me. For so long, I've had to be aware of everything around me, always ready to react or defend myself. But being with Finn, feeling his strength and steadiness, allows me to relax into the dance.

By the third song, I'm actually enjoying myself. We're not winning any dance contests, but we're moving together, and Finn's been right about the other dancers. Some are clearly experienced, spinning and dipping with practiced ease, but plenty of others are just having fun, laughing when they mess up and jumping right back in.

"See that couple over there?" Finn nods toward an elderly pair who are dancing like they've been doing it for decades. "That's Chuck and Betty Morrison. They've been coming to these dances for as long as I can remember."

I watch them move together with such natural rhythm, such obvious joy in each other's company. "They look happy."

"They are. Harold always says dancing is what keeps their marriage strong. Forces them to work together and have fun doing it," Finn says, his voice wistful.

"Is that what you want someday? That kind of partnership?"

"Yeah," he says quietly, his eyes meeting mine. "I do."

His eyes hold mine, and my heart starts to race. Neither of us looks away. When the band slows things down for the next song, suddenly Finn's arms are around me properly, my head resting against his chest as we sway together. I can hear his heartbeat through his shirt, steady and strong. His hand strokes my back gently, and I feel safer than I have in years.

"Thank you for bringing me tonight," I murmur against his chest.

"Thank you for saying yes," he replies, his voice rumbling under my ear. "I love dancing with you."

We dance through two more slow songs, barely moving, just holding each other. When the band picks up the tempo again, Finn pulls back to look at me.

"Want to try a spin?" he asks with a mischievous grin.

"I don't know . . ."

"Trust me."

And I do. I trust him completely as he guides me through a simple turn, laughing when I get dizzy and stumble into him. His hands steady me, and we're very close, his face inches from mine.

For a moment, the music and the other dancers fade away. It's just us, breathing the same air, his eyes searching mine.

"Patty," he says softly.

"Yeah?"

"I'm really glad you moved to Piney Brook."

"Me too," I whisper.

He smiles and spins me again, this time successfully, and we fall back into the rhythm of the dance. As the evening continues, I find myself relaxing more and more. People introduce themselves, compliment Finn on bringing such a lovely date, and include me in conversations like I've always been part of this community.

Mrs. Richards invites me to join the church's monthly potluck dinner. A younger woman named Jennifer asks if I'd be interested in their book club. An older gentleman tells me I remind him of his daughter and insists on showing me pictures.

When the band announces the last dance of the evening, Finn stands and offers me his hand. "One more?"

The final song is slow and sweet, and as we move together on the dance floor, I realize our relationship has shifted tonight. This isn't just dating anymore. This feels like it could be permanent if I'm brave enough to let it.

As we drive home, I rest my head against the truck window and watch the dark countryside pass by. Finn's hand finds mine across the console, his thumb tracing gentle circles on my palm.

"Penny for your thoughts," he says softly.

"Just thinking about tonight," I say. "It was nice to just have fun. To feel like I belonged."

"You do belong," he says, squeezing my hand.

When he walks me to my door, he doesn't immediately say goodnight. Instead, he takes both my hands in his and looks at me with an expression I've never seen before.

"Tonight was perfect. You're perfect," he says.

He kisses my forehead gently, lingering for a moment before stepping back.

"Sweet dreams," he murmurs.

"You too."

As I watch him drive away, I touch the spot where his lips brushed my skin.

I think I'm falling in love with Finn Miller.

CHAPTER TEN

Finn

I'm still smiling as I drive away from Patty's apartment, the memory of her in my arms during that last dance replaying in my head. She looked radiant tonight.

My phone rings as I turn onto the main road back to the ranch. Cooper's name flashes on the screen.

"Hey," I answer, putting him on speaker.

"How was the barn dance?" he asks without preamble. "Alec mentioned you were taking Patty tonight."

"It was . . ." I pause, trying to find the right words. "Really good. She loved it."

"That's great, man. She seems like a keeper."

"Yeah," I say, the word carrying more weight than Cooper probably realizes. "She really is."

"You sound happy," Cooper says. "Happy and weird. What did she do to you, dude? You're not yourself."

He's right. I do feel different. Tonight, watching Patty laugh as she learned to two-step, seeing how naturally she fit in with people I've known my whole life, something clicked into place. This isn't just about Uncle Harry's stipulations, or finding a convenient wife to secure my inheritance.

This is about the person I want to spend my life with.

"Cooper," I say, making a decision that feels both terrifying and absolutely right. "I need to ask you a question."

"Shoot."

"What would you think if I walked away from the ranch?"

There's a long pause on the other end of the line. "What do you mean, 'walked away?'"

I pull over to the side of the road, needing to focus on this conversation. "I mean what if I told Uncle Harry I don't want it anymore? What if I let him sell it to someone else?"

"Finn, what are you talking about? You've wanted that ranch your entire life."

"I know. But things have changed."

"Because of Patty?"

"Because of how I feel about Patty." I run a hand through my hair, trying to organize my thoughts. "Cooper, I'm falling in love with her. Really, completely in love. And I can't stand the thought that she might think my feelings for her have anything to do with Uncle Harry's requirement."

"So tell her about the requirement," Cooper says, like it's obvious.

"And have her think I've been dating her to solve my inheritance problem? That I see her as a convenient solution instead of the woman I'm crazy about?"

"But that's not why you're dating her."

"No, it's not. But how would she know that? How would anyone know that?" I lean back against the headrest, staring up at the star-filled sky. "Tonight, watching her dance, seeing how happy she was . . . Cooper, I realized I'd rather lose the ranch and keep her than risk losing her to save the ranch."

Another long pause. "Wow. You really are in love."

"I am. And I think she might be falling for me too, but she's been hurt before. She's careful about trusting people. If I tell her about Uncle Harry's ultimatum now, she'll think our entire relationship has been built on a lie."

"Has it been?"

"No! I asked her out because I couldn't stop thinking about her. I've been pursuing her because she makes me happy. The inheritance thing just . . . complicated the timing."

"Okay, so let's think about this logically," Cooper says, slipping into his problem-solving mode. "What exactly are you proposing?"

"I'll sit down with Uncle Harry tomorrow and tell him I'm not interested in the ranch. That he should go ahead and sell it. That way, when I eventually tell Patty how I feel about her, she'll know it has nothing to do with inheriting anything."

"And then what? You move back to Montana? Start over somewhere else?"

The thought of leaving Arkansas for good, walking away from the land I've loved my whole life, makes my chest ache. But the thought of losing Patty makes it hurt worse.

"I don't know," I admit. "Maybe. Or maybe I'll stay here and start a small farm of my own. Work for someone else. Whatever it takes to build a life with her."

"Finn," Cooper says, "are you sure you're thinking clearly? This is a huge decision."

"I've never been more sure of anything in my life."

"What about Caleb and Colton? Holly? Have you talked to them about this?"

"Not yet."

"Call them. Tonight. You shouldn't make a decision this big without letting everyone know."

"What do you think?"

Cooper's quiet for a long moment. "I think I've never heard you talk about a woman the way you talk about Patty. And I've also never heard you consider giving up the ranch for anything or anyone. So either you've lost your mind, or this is the real deal."

"It's the real deal," I say without hesitation.

"Then maybe losing the ranch wouldn't be the worst thing in the world. Family land is a great blessing, but building your own family is more important."

That's what I'd be doing. Building my own family. With Patty. It feels right.

"Thanks, Coop."

"Call everyone else. Then get some sleep. For what it's worth, I think you're making the right choice. Patty seems like the kind of woman worth taking risks for."

After we hang up, I sit in my truck for a while, watching the stars and thinking. Memories of the night flow through my mind like a home movie. Patty's face lighting up when Mrs. Richards invited her to the church potluck. How natural she looked spinning in my arms. The moment during our last dance when she looked up at me like I was her whole world.

I've spent my entire adult life working toward taking over Apple Blossom Ranch. It's been my goal, my identity, my future. But tonight made me realize that futures can change. Turns out, the thing I thought I wanted isn't nearly as important as the one I never saw coming.

My phone rings again. Caleb this time.

"Cooper called me," he says immediately. "Tell me you're not really thinking about walking away from the ranch."

"I am thinking about it. Seriously."

"Because of a woman you've known for a few weeks?"

"Because of the woman I want to spend the rest of my life with," I say. "Caleb, I know how it sounds. But I need you to understand this. Tonight, I realized that if I had to choose between the ranch and Patty, I'd choose her every time."

"That's . . ." He pauses. "Actually really romantic. And also completely insane."

I laugh. "Thanks for the vote of confidence."

"I'm not saying don't do it. I'm saying make sure you've thought it through. Have you considered just telling her the truth about Uncle Harry's requirement? She might surprise you."

"And she might run. She's been hurt before, Caleb. She's careful about trusting people. If I tell her now that our entire relationship started while I had this deadline hanging over my head, she'll think I've been using her."

"Don't you think she'll find out about it anyway?"

"Maybe, but at least this way, when the truth comes out, there won't be any doubt where my priorities are."

Caleb is quiet for a moment. "By giving up the ranch first you're removing any chance for suspicion about your motives."

"Exactly."

"It's a grand gesture," he admits. "Probably the most romantic thing I've ever heard. But Finn, are you sure you won't regret it? That ranch has been in our family for three generations."

"And maybe it's time for it to go to a family that can appreciate it together," I say, echoing Uncle Harry's words. "Besides, who says I can't build something new? Start my own legacy with Patty?"

"You really love her."

"I really do."

"Then I support you," Caleb says. "The ranch is just land. Love is . . . everything else. I'll tell the others. All I ask is you take some time before you tell Uncle Harry. Make sure this is really what you want."

After we hang up, I'm filled with a sense of peace I haven't felt in weeks. The decision feels right. More than right. It feels like the only choice I can live with.

CHAPTER ELEVEN

Patty

The knock on my apartment door comes at exactly seven on Wednesday morning. I grab my purse and the covered dish I made last night, take a deep breath, and open the door to find Finn waiting with a smile that makes my stomach flutter.

"Ready for your first day as a ranch cook?" he asks, taking the dish from my hands.

"As ready as I'll ever be," I reply, locking the door behind me. "I made apple crisp again. I figured it was a safe bet to win Margaret over."

"She will love that." He opens the passenger door of his truck for me. "She's excited to have help. And I'm excited to have you there."

The drive to Apple Blossom Ranch takes us through rolling hills dotted with other farms. Finn tells me stories about the kids he knew who grew up in each one. About the Kinards who had a pool where Finn slipped and had to get six stitches in his chin. And the Edwards boys who used to shoot each other with BB guns until their mom had to dig one out of Shawn's back.

Finn asks about my childhood, and I tell him about the time when I was ten and I wanted to surprise my grandma with a birthday cake and ended up splattering batter all over the kitchen, including the ceiling. When she woke up, she was definitely surprised, but not in the way I'd hoped.

When we turn down the gravel drive marked by the weathered wooden sign, I'm struck by how different the place looks during harvest season. There are trucks parked near the equipment barn, and I can see people moving through the orchard rows with ladders and canvas bags.

Margaret emerges from the house before Finn has even parked, wiping her hands on an apron and beaming at us.

"Patty! Perfect timing. I just put on a fresh pot of coffee."

"Thank you for letting me help," I say, climbing out of the truck. "I'm nervous but excited."

"Nervous is normal," Margaret laughs. "Though you might feel differently after a few hours of prep work. Come on, let me show you around the kitchen properly."

Finn carries my apple crisp to the house, gives me a quick kiss on the cheek, and heads back toward the orchard. "Have fun, you two. Try not to work too hard."

The farmhouse kitchen takes my breath away. Every surface seems to be in use, with large pots and huge containers of ingredients organized along the counter. It's clear Margaret has this operation down to a science.

"You feed all the workers out of this kitchen?" I ask, taking it all in.

Margaret grins. "The trick is planning ahead and keeping things simple. The crew doesn't expect fancy meals, just good, filling food."

She walks me through the planned menu for the week, showing me where everything's stored and explaining the rhythm of meal prep. It's more organized than the diner kitchen, and there's a homey feeling here that even the scratched countertops and mismatched pots seem to add to.

"The crew eats breakfast and dinner in the bunkhouse dining room," Margaret explains, "but lunch is usually packed and eaten in the orchard. Sandwiches, fruit, plenty of water."

"What can I do to help today?" I ask, already rolling up my sleeves.

"Well, we could get started on tomorrow's bread. I usually bake fresh every other day during harvest."

For the next two hours, Margaret teaches me her bread recipe while we chat about everything from gardening to small-town gossip. Her hands move with practiced ease as she demonstrates how to work the bread, and I find myself relaxing in a way I haven't in a long time.

"You're a natural," she says, watching me work my own batch of dough. "Have you thought about cooking professionally?"

I pause in my kneading. "Not really. I enjoy it, but I've never had formal training."

"Some of the best cooks I know learned from their grandmothers," Margaret says kindly. "Passion matters more than credentials."

The back door opens, and Finn walks in with dirt on his clothes and tree leaves in his hair. His face lights up when he sees me, and my heart does that familiar skip.

"How's the kitchen training going?" he asks, washing his hands at the sink.

"Your aunt is a wonderful teacher," I tell him. "I think I'm getting the hang of it."

"Margaret could teach anyone to cook," Finn says, snagging a piece of bread from yesterday's loaf. "She's been feeding this family for decades."

"Flattery will get you everywhere," Margaret teases, swatting at him with a dish towel. "You're still not getting lunch early."

Finn grins and heads back outside. The casual way he fits into this space, the easy affection between him and Margaret, makes warmth settle in my chest.

"Finn's never brought a woman to the ranch during harvest season before," Margaret says quietly once he's gone.

"Oh." I'm not sure what to say to that. "Is that significant?"

"Harvest is sacred time for the Miller men," Margaret explains, returning to her bread dough. "It's when this place becomes completely focused on the work. The fact that Finn wants you here tells me everything I need to know about how he feels."

Her words make my chest tight with emotion. I've spent so many years feeling like I didn't belong anywhere, always on the outside looking in. The idea that Finn wants me to be involved in this important part of his life is overwhelming in the best way.

Around noon, we start preparing lunch for the crew. Margaret has laid out the ingredients so we can work as an assembly line. We prepare sandwiches, fruit, cookies, and a thermos of sweet tea for each worker. I fall into the rhythm easily, surprising myself with how natural it feels.

"Patty!" a familiar voice calls from the doorway. I turn to see Alec, Finn's longtime friend and the orchard foreman, grinning at me, his clothes dusty from the field. "So you're the one who's got our boss walking around with a permanent smile."

"Alec," Margaret warns, though she's smiling too.

"I'm just saying hello," Alec protests, accepting a packed lunch from me. "And to thank you. Finn's been a lot more pleasant to work with lately."

Before I can respond, Miguel appears in the kitchen. "Don't mind Alec," he says. "He doesn't have a filter."

"I have a filter," Alec argues. "I just choose not to use it most of the time."

The easy banter between the men reminds me of what I've been missing. Family. The chosen family that comes from shared experiences and genuine care for each other.

"You boys take your lunch and get back to work," Margaret says, shooing them toward the door. "And tell the crew to send their thermoses back when they're done."

After lunch is distributed, Margaret and I start prep work for dinner. She teaches me how to season the large roasts that will feed the crew, and I help her prep vegetables for tomorrow's soup. The work is more satisfying than I had expected—creating food that will nourish people who are working hard.

"Can I ask you a question?" I say as we work side by side peeling potatoes.

"Of course, dear."

"How long have you been part of this family?"

Margaret's smile turns wistful. "Feels like forever since Fred and I came to work for Harry. Fred was Harry's best friend from childhood, and when Harry needed a foreman, he asked us to come help run the ranch. After Fred passed on, I didn't want to leave."

"And now you and Harry are married."

"Life has a funny way of working out," Margaret agrees. "I never expected to find love again at my age, though sometimes the heart surprises you."

Her words resonate deeper than I think she realizes. A few months ago, I would have said I was done with love, done with trusting anyone else with my heart. Being here, being part of this family's life, makes me wonder if I was wrong.

"Finn's a good man," Margaret says, as if reading my thoughts. "He's got his father's heart and his uncle's work ethic. Any woman would be lucky to have him."

"I think I'm the lucky one," I admit quietly.

Margaret pauses in her peeling to look at me directly. "Honey, from what I can see, you're both pretty lucky."

The afternoon passes quickly as we prepare for the evening meal. Margaret teaches me how to make her famous cornbread and shows me the trick to getting the timing right when cooking for such a large group. By the time the crew starts trickling in for dinner, I feel like I'm actually contributing in a meaningful way.

Finn appears in the kitchen doorway as we're putting the finishing touches on the meal. He's cleaned up and changed clothes, and the look on his face as he watches me makes my stomach flutter.

"How was your first day as a ranch cook?" he asks.

"Exhausting," I admit. "Also really good."

"She's a pro already," Margaret says, beaming with pride. "She's a quick study and not afraid to work hard. Having her help is a blessing."

The crew gathers around the long tables in the bunkhouse dining room, and I help Margaret serve the meal family-style. The men are polite and appreciative, thanking us for the food and complimenting the cornbread. It's different from serving at the diner, more personal.

"Miss Patty," one of the older crew members says as I refill his sweet tea, "this cornbread is the best I've had since my mama's."

The compliment warms me more than it should. "Thank you. Margaret taught me her secret."

"Well, you learned good," he says with a grin.

After dinner, while Margaret organizes the cleanup, Finn pulls me aside.

"Want to walk down to the pond?" he asks. "I could use some quiet after all the noise today."

"That sounds perfect."

We walk through the orchard as the sun sets, painting the sky in brilliant colors. The air is crisp with autumn, and the scent of ripening apples surrounds us. Finn's hand finds mine naturally, and I feel a sense of rightness settle over me.

"Thank you for today," he says as we reach the small pond at the edge of the property. "Having you here made everything better."

"I loved it," I tell him honestly. "Your family is wonderful. Margaret treated me like I belonged from the moment I walked in."

"You do belong," Finn says, stopping to face me. "At least, I hope you feel that way."

There's a weight in his voice that makes me study his face more carefully. "Is everything okay?"

"More than okay," he says quickly. "Being with you, having you here . . . it's everything I didn't know I wanted."

The intensity in his eyes makes my heart race. "Finn . . ."

"I know we haven't known each other long," he continues, "but I need you to know how I feel. You're becoming someone I can't imagine my life without."

The declaration takes my breath away. Part of me wants to say the words back, to tell him I feel the same way. Another part, the part that's been hurt before, holds back.

"I . . . really like you too," I whisper instead. "You scare me in the best way."

"I scare you?"

I take a deep breath. "You make me want things I thought I'd given up on. A real relationship. A future. Someone to share my life with."

Finn's hands cup my face gently. "You can have all of that, Patty. *We* can have that."

He brushes his lips across my forehead in a gesture so sweet it hurts. Standing there by the pond as darkness settles around us, I let myself think that maybe I deserve this kind of happiness.

"I should get you home," Finn says eventually, though he doesn't sound like he wants to.

"Probably," I agree, making no move to step away from him.

On the drive back to town, we're both quiet, lost in our own thoughts. When Finn walks me to my door, I turn to face him, my hand on the doorknob.

"Thank you for including me today," I say. "For making me feel like part of this."

"Thank you for saying yes," he replies. "I'll see you Sunday?"

"Definitely."

He kisses my cheek softly, and I watch from my window as he drives away. As I get ready for bed, I think about the day, about how well I've taken to the rhythm of the ranch, about how Finn's family welcomed me without hesitation.

For the first time in years, I'm living instead of just surviving. And it feels wonderful.

CHAPTER TWELVE

Finn

String lights twinkle between the apple trees, casting a warm glow over the makeshift celebration area we've set up in the main orchard. The Harvest Festival at Apple Blossom Ranch is in full swing, marking the halfway point of our picking season. Tables covered with food stretch under the oak tree, and the sound of laughter mingles with acoustic guitar music Sara, one of the newer workers, is playing.

I adjust my collar and scan the crowd for Patty. She's been helping Margaret serve food to the mix of crew members and Barberville folks who've come out for the evening. This festival has been a ranch tradition for decades, Uncle Harry's way of saying thank you to the community that supports us and the workers who make harvest possible.

The scent of Margaret's famous chili and fresh cornbread drifts through the evening air, mixing with the sweet smell of ripe apples still hanging on nearby branches. Kids from Barberville run between the trees while their parents chat with our crew. It's exactly the kind of night that makes me love this place even more.

"Finn!"

I turn to see Patty approaching with a steaming bowl in her hands and that smile that never fails to make my heart skip. She's wearing a soft blue sweater and jeans, her hair loose around her shoulders. After two weeks of seeing her helping Margaret every few days, she looks completely at home here.

"Margaret sent me to make sure you're eating," she says, offering me the bowl. "She says you've been too busy playing host to take care of yourself."

"Margaret worries too much," I say, accepting the chili gratefully. "How are you enjoying your first ranch festival?"

"It's wonderful," she replies, her eyes bright with happiness. "I love seeing everyone together like this. It feels like a real community celebration."

We find a spot on a hay bale someone's dragged over to serve as seating. Across the clearing, Clarabelle—the most spoiled cow on the ranch—chews thoughtfully beside the fence, wearing a flower crown that Dorothy Chen insisted on placing on her head. "Duchess Clarabelle Mooington" suits her perfectly.

Around us, the festival continues with kids giggling and running everywhere. Miguel, our crew leader, is telling stories in rapid Spanish to a group of kids who don't understand a word, yet hang on every gesture. Sara is busy teaching guitar to anyone willing to learn.

"This is what I imagined when I was a kid thinking about running this place," I admit, watching a group of teenagers from Barberville learn to square dance from some of the older crew members. "The ranch bringing people together."

"You're good at it," Patty observes. "I've watched you tonight, making sure everyone feels welcome, checking on the families with young kids, helping set up the music area. You care about these people."

Her words warm me more than the chili. "They're what makes this place special. The land is beautiful, and the work is satisfying, but without the community around it, it would just be a job."

"Finn! There you are!" calls a familiar voice. We turn to see Dorothy Chen approaching—Margaret's best friend since childhood. She's a spry woman in her seventies with silver hair and sharp eyes that miss nothing. "I've been looking for you to say hello."

"Mrs. Chen." I stand to greet her. "I'm so glad you could make it. This is Patty Walsh. Patty, this is Dorothy Chen. She and Margaret have been friends since they were in diapers."

"Oh, stop," Dorothy laughs, settling beside us. "We weren't that young when we met. It was kindergarten." She turns to Patty with obvious interest. "So you're the young woman who's got Margaret so excited. She can't stop talking about you."

Patty blushes. "Margaret's been wonderful to work with. She's taught me so much."

"Well, Margaret's a good judge of character, and she clearly thinks the world of you." Dorothy's eyes twinkle as she looks between us. "She also mentioned you two make quite the pair. Says it's nice to see Finn so happy."

I feel heat creep up my neck. "Mrs. Chen . . ."

"What? I'm just making conversation." She pats Patty's knee conspiratorially. "Margaret and I have been watching the Miller boys grow up for years. We know when one of them is smitten."

Before I can protest further, Dorothy spots someone else she wants to greet and excuses herself with a knowing smile. Patty watches her go with amusement.

"Smitten?" she teases, bumping my shoulder.

"Margaret talks too much," I mutter, though I'm grinning.

The evening continues with easy companionship. We sample Margaret's desserts, watch people dancing, and chat with workers and townspeople. Patty fits in seamlessly, and I find myself imagining many more nights like this, with her beside me as we host the community we both care about.

As the crowd begins to thin and families with young children start heading home, Patty and I help with cleanup. We're stacking empty serving dishes when she pauses, looking out over the orchard where a few couples are still swaying to the soft guitar music.

"This is magical," she says quietly. "I can see why you love it here so much."

She looks at this place with such appreciation it makes my chest ache with longing. Standing here in the orchard with string lights casting shadows between the trees, surrounded by the lingering warmth of community celebration, I realize I can't hold back the truth any longer.

"Patty—" I start, then stop. There's so much I want to tell her, but I need to talk to Uncle Harry first.

She looks at me, sensing the shift in my tone. "What is it?"

"Nothing," I say, chickening out. "You look beautiful."

"Thank you," she says, eyeing me like she knows I wanted to say something more serious.

Just then, Alec comes up, slightly out of breath from herding Clarabelle back to the cow pasture. "Great party," he says to me, then turns to Patty. "Did you have fun dancing with Finn?"

"I did," she says warmly, lacing her fingers through mine. "Though Finn's toes might disagree. I still can't get some of the more complicated steps down."

Alec laughs. "You'll have plenty of time to practice after next month."

"Next month?" she asks, smiling.

I freeze and Patty glances over at me, but her eyes don't linger.

"Yeah, it'll have to be next month if Finn's going to meet the marriage requirement."

Patty goes completely still beside me.

"What marriage requirement?" she asks, her voice quiet.

Alec's face drains of color as he realizes what he let slip. "I . . . uh . . ." He looks at me apologetically.

"Alec," I say, my voice tight.

But it's too late. Patty takes a step back from me, her expression changing from confusion to hurt.

"What is he talking about, Finn?" she repeats, her pitch rising.

"Uncle Harry thinks running a place this size alone is too much for one man alone. That I need a partner to share the responsibility." The words come easier now that I've started. "He says he doesn't want me to miss out on a relationship because I'm too busy with the ranch, and he's given me until the end of harvest season to figure it out or he'll sell."

"That's only a few more weeks," she says.

"I know." I turn to face her fully, needing her to see the truth in my eyes. "Patty, I need you to understand. When we first met, I was drawn to you. I asked you out because I wanted to get to know you better. When Uncle Harry told me about his condition, I was upset, but the more I thought about it. About you. I thought maybe . . ."

Her face goes completely still. I watch the color drain from her cheeks as the words sink in.

"You thought maybe what?" Her voice is barely a whisper.

"That what we had could work for both of us," I finish lamely. "But my feelings for you are real, Patty. I fell in love with you. With your kindness and strength, with how you make this place feel like home. But the ranch doesn't matter to me anymore. You are more important to me. Wherever you are is home to me now. I decided I'm going to turn down the offer—"

She takes several steps back from me. "You've been evaluating me this entire time? Like I was some kind of business transaction?"

"No, that's not . . ."

"So when you asked me out, when you brought me here . . ." Her voice is getting shakier with each word. "You were thinking about how I could solve your problem?"

"Patty, please listen—"

"I trusted you." The words come out broken, and I can see her hands trembling. "I let myself believe that someone could actually care about me for who I am, not for what I could provide."

The pain in her voice cuts through me like a blade. "I do care about you. I love you."

"Do you?" She wraps her arms around herself protectively. "Or do you love the idea of having a convenient wife who comes with good references from Margaret?"

"That's not fair."

"Fair?" Her laugh is bitter. "You want to talk about fair? You lied to me, Finn. For weeks. You let me think this was real when you had an agenda from day one."

"My feelings are real. I've never felt this way about anyone ever before," I insist, standing up and taking a step toward her. She immediately steps back, and the rejection stings.

"How am I supposed to believe that? How am I supposed to trust anything you've said when our entire relationship started with you lying to me?"

"I never lied."

"Lies of omission are still lies." Her voice is stronger now, anger mixing with the hurt. "You let me fall for you while hiding the fact that you needed a wife so you could get your inheritance. You brought me into your family, made me feel like I belonged, all while keeping this massive secret."

The accusation hits home because she's right. I did hide it. I did let her get attached while keeping my true situation a secret.

"I was going to tell you," I say weakly.

"When? After we were married? After I'd already committed my life to solving *your* problem?"

I don't have a good answer for that.

She's quiet for a long moment, staring at the ground. When she finally looks up, there are tears streaming down her face.

"I need to go," she says.

"Patty, please. Let me explain."

"There's nothing to explain. You made your choice when you decided to ask me out under false pretences instead of being honest from the beginning." She starts walking toward her car.

"Don't leave like this, please!" I call after her. "We can work through this."

She stops and turns back to me, and the look on her face makes my chest ache.

"The worst part is that I was starting to believe I deserved good things. That maybe I could have a real relationship with someone who saw me as more than just useful." She shakes her head. "I should've known better."

"You do deserve good things. This *is* good, what we have—"

"What we have is built on a lie." She opens her car door. "I can't do this, Finn. I won't be someone's convenient solution again."

The word stops me cold. "Patty, what do you mean?"

She pauses, her hand on the door frame. "My ex-husband married me because I was useful too. Because I could cook and clean and make him look good to his family. When I finally got away, I swore I'd never let anyone use me like that again."

The pain in her voice as she's comparing me to the man who hurt her makes me feel sick.

"I'm not like him," I say desperately.

"Aren't you?" She gets in the car and rolls down the window. "You both saw what I could do for you before you saw who I was."

I watch helplessly as she starts the engine. "Patty, please. Don't do this. Don't throw away what we have because of how it started."

"What we have was never real," she says quietly. "At least not for you."

"That's not . . ." I can't get the words out. It feels like this is the most important conversation of my life. "Patty, I don't want the ranch anymore. I only want you. If and when we get married will be up to you. I'll wait until you're ready. I only asked you out because I already had you on my mind. I would have asked you out eventually without any nudging. This thing about the ranch just kickstarted things. But that doesn't make how I feel any less real." As the words leave my mouth, I can hear how weak and whiny they sound. If I don't buy it, there's no way Patty will.

"How am I supposed to know the difference, Finn?" She sighs and slides the gearshift into drive. "I . . . I need some time."

She drives away without another word, leaving me standing alone in the orchard. The string lights have all been taken down, and the tables cleared away. The celebration is over, and so, it seems, is everything I thought I was building with Patty.

I stand there for a long time, replaying the conversation and hating myself for every choice I made that led to this moment. She's right to be angry, to feel betrayed. I did exactly what I swore I wouldn't do—I hurt the woman I love by being a coward about the truth.

The worst part isn't losing the ranch. It's knowing that I've broken her trust, and trust isn't an easy thing to earn back. I'll have to find a way, though, because I can't imagine life without this woman.

Time.

She asked for time.

The question is whether I can ever prove to her what she means to me, or if I've lost her forever.

CHAPTER THIRTEEN

Patty

I sit in my car in Ruth's driveway for a full ten minutes after turning off the engine, staring at the steering wheel and trying to make sense of what just happened. My hands are still shaking, and there's a hollow ache in my chest that feels too big for my body to contain.

"When we first met, I was drawn to you."

The words should be comforting. They should prove that Finn's feelings are real, that I wasn't just some convenient solution to his problem. Instead, they make everything worse because they mean he already liked me when he decided to start calculating how I could fit into his plans.

I finally force myself out of the car and up the steps to my apartment. The space feels smaller tonight, the silence pressing in around me. I drop my purse by the door and sink onto my small couch, pulling a throw pillow against my chest like armor.

The worst part isn't even that he didn't tell me about Uncle Harry's condition. It's that he let me fall in love with him while keeping such a huge secret. Every moment we shared, every time he held my hand, there was this secret sitting between us that I didn't know existed.

I think about Klive, and how he pursued me with flowers and sweet words, making me feel like the most important person in the world. It wasn't until after we were married, and he started hurting me, that I realized I'd been evaluated for my usefulness as a wife. He hadn't loved me for who I was. The cooking, the cleaning, how I made him look good to his family and colleagues. I was a careful selection, not a choice of the heart. And every time I failed . . .

Is that what this is, too? Did Finn look at me and see someone who could cook for his crew, fit into his family, and solve his inheritance problem?

But even as the thought forms, I know it's not entirely fair. The sweet expression Finn gets when he looks at me when he thinks I'm not watching, the gentle way he touches my face, the pride in his voice when he introduces me to people. Those things feel real—Klive's attention never did.

My phone buzzes on the coffee table.

Anne: *How was the festival? Did you have fun?*

I stare at the message for a long time before answering.

Me: *It was complicated. Can we talk tomorrow?*

Her response comes immediately.

Anne: *Of course. You okay?*

Me: *I think so. Just processing some things.*

Anne: *Call me if you need me tonight. I mean it.*

The kindness in her words makes my eyes burn with tears I've been holding back. This is what I have in Piney Brook that I never had with

Klive. Real friends who care about me without wanting anything in return. A job where I'm valued. A life I've built for myself.

The question is whether Finn can be part of that life, or if his secret has poisoned our relationship.

I get ready for bed mechanically, washing my face and brushing my teeth while my mind replays the entire evening. The sweet way Finn looked when he told me he loved me, the pain in his voice when I walked away, his pleading eyes when he said that wherever I am is home.

Was that true? Or did he say it because he was desperate?

Sleep doesn't come easily. I toss and turn, my mind circling through the same questions over and over. By the time my alarm goes off for my early shift at the diner, I feel like I've been hit by a truck.

Ms. Daisy takes one look at me when I walk in and immediately puts the coffee pot on. "Rough night, honey?"

"Something like that." I tie my apron with trembling fingers. "I'll be fine once I get moving."

"Mm-hmm." She doesn't sound convinced. "Well, it's Tuesday, so it should be slow until the lunch rush. Good day for thinking through whatever's got you looking like you wrestled a bear."

The morning passes in a blur of coffee refills and breakfast orders. I'm grateful for the routine, the familiar rhythm of work that requires just enough attention to keep my darker thoughts at bay. It's not until Anne slides onto a counter stool around ten that I realize I've been dreading this conversation as much as I've been needing it.

"You look terrible," she says without preamble.

"Thanks. That's exactly what every woman wants to hear."

"I'm serious, Patty. What happened last night?"

I glance around the nearly empty diner, then pour Anne a cup of coffee and lean against the counter. "I found out about a secret that Finn's been keeping from me."

Anne settles on her stool, wrapping her hands around the warm mug. "What kind of secret?"

"His uncle won't pass the ranch on to him unless he's married. He has about four weeks to figure it out, or Harry's going to sell."

"Oh." Anne processes this for a moment. "And you're upset because . . . ?"

"Because he's known about this condition the whole time we've been seeing each other and never told me. Because he was drawn to me first, but he didn't ask me out until after he learned about Uncle Harry's requirement." The words come out faster now, the hurt and anger I've been holding back spilling over. "He said he asked me out for real reasons, but he was already thinking about how I could solve his problem."

Anne's quiet for a long moment, stirring her coffee thoughtfully. "Has he told you he loves you?"

"Yes."

"Do you believe him?"

The question stops me cold. "I . . . I don't know. I want to. But how can I trust my own judgment when I was so wrong about Klive?"

"Honey," Anne says gently, "Finn is not Klive."

"How do you know that?"

"Because I've watched you since you moved here." Anne reaches across the counter to squeeze my hand. "When you first arrived, you were so careful, so guarded. You jumped at loud noises and apologized for everything. With Finn, you laugh. You argue with him about silly things. You're yourself."

She's right. I am different with Finn. More relaxed, more confident. More like the person I used to be before Klive convinced me I wasn't enough.

"But he still lied to me," I say weakly.

"Did he? Or did he just not know how to tell you something that would sound terrible no matter how he said it?" Anne tilts her head. "Think about it, Patty. How would you have reacted if he'd told you about the marriage requirement on your second date? Would you have given him a chance to prove his feelings were real?"

I consider this. Honestly, I probably would've run. I would have panicked and shut down completely.

"Probably not," I admit.

"So he was stuck between telling you too early and scaring you off, or waiting too long and making you feel deceived." Anne's voice is gentle but firm. "Either way, he was going to hurt you. At least this way, you got to know each other first. You got to build a real connection before the pressure of his situation complicated things."

"You think what we have is real?"

"I think the question is what you think." Anne studies my face carefully. "Do you love him?"

The answer comes without hesitation. "Yes."

"Then maybe the question isn't whether he handled this perfectly. Maybe it's whether you're willing to work through it together."

Before I can respond, the bell above the door chimes. I look up to see Finn walking in, and my heart immediately starts racing. He looks like he slept about as well as I did, his hair rumpled, dark circles under his eyes.

Our eyes meet across the diner, and for a moment neither of us moves. Then he walks slowly to the counter, stopping a careful distance away.

"Hi," he says quietly.

"Hi."

Anne looks between us, then stands up. "I should get back to the salon. Patty, think about what I said, okay?"

She squeezes my shoulder and leaves, the bell chiming again in her wake.

Finn and I stand in uncomfortable silence for a moment. Finally, he speaks.

"I came to apologize. Not to pressure you or ask for anything, just to say I'm sorry. I handled everything wrong, and I hurt you. That's the last thing I ever wanted to do."

His voice is rough with exhaustion and regret, and I can see the sincerity in his eyes. This isn't a calculated move or a manipulation. This is a man who made a mistake and is genuinely sorry for it.

"I know," I say softly. "I'm sorry too. For comparing you to him. That wasn't fair."

"It was fair," Finn says immediately. "You have every right to protect yourself. I gave you reason to doubt me."

My eyes prick with tears. He doesn't argue, or try to convince me to forgive him, just shows he understands. Klive never would have validated my feelings like that. It makes me want to forgive him, to trust again, but I've been burned before.

"I need more time," I tell him. "To think about everything and figure out what I want."

"Take all the time you need," he says. "I'll wait."

"What about Uncle Harry's deadline?"

Finn's expression grows serious. "I meant what I said last night. I'd rather lose the ranch than lose you, so I was planning to tell Uncle

Harry—today, in fact—to sell the ranch. I didn't want this hanging over us. Seems I messed up anyway."

The pressure I've felt under eases slightly.

"Will you still come to the ranch tomorrow?" he asks hesitantly. "Margaret's been looking forward to teaching you her apple pie recipe. I don't want my mistakes to affect your friendship with her. Plus, I think Clarabelle misses you. Alec found her trying to get into the kitchen this morning."

I can't help the chuckle that bubbles up. "She's rotten," I say. Do I want to go back to the ranch, though? The fact that he's thinking about my relationship with Margaret, that he's not trying to use it as leverage to get me back, tells me that he is considerate of me, and compassionate.

"I'll come," I say. "For Margaret."

"Thank you." He starts to leave, then turns back. "Patty? I would have proposed even if I only had a bicycle to my name. What I feel for you has nothing to do with the ranch."

He leaves before I can respond, the bell chiming one final time. I stand there holding onto his words, turning them over in my mind like stones I'm trying to polish smooth.

Anne was right, Finn isn't Klive. The question now is whether I'm brave enough to trust that difference.

CHAPTER FOURTEEN

Finn

I 've been staring at my phone for twenty minutes, typing and deleting the same text message to Patty over and over again. Each version sounds either too desperate, too casual, or too much like I'm trying to explain myself when she asked for time to think.

Finally, I toss the phone onto my nightstand and scrub my hands over my face. It's barely past six in the morning, and I've been awake since three, replaying every word of our conversation at the festival. The look on her face when she realized I'd kept Uncle Harry's condition from her. How she compared me to her ex-husband.

The sadness in her voice when she said she needed time.

I should respect that. I *am* respecting that. But sitting here doing nothing while the woman I love questions how I feel about her is torture.

There's a soft knock on my bedroom door. "Finn? You awake?" Uncle Harry's voice drifts through the wood.

"Yeah, come in."

He opens the door carrying two steaming mugs of coffee, and I've never been more grateful for his early-rising habits. He hands me one and settles in the chair by my window.

"Rough night?" he asks, though his tone suggests he already knows the answer.

"You could say that." I take a sip of the coffee, black and strong enough to wake the dead. "Did Margaret tell you what happened?"

"She mentioned you and Patty had a difficult conversation." Uncle Harry studies my face carefully. "Want to talk about it?"

I lean back against my headboard, suddenly feeling exhausted despite the caffeine. "She found out about the marriage condition. She didn't take it well."

"I see." He's quiet for a moment. "What do you mean didn't she take it well?"

"She thinks I've been using her. Evaluating her for how well she'd fit into my life instead of actually caring about her." The words taste bitter as I say them.

Uncle Harry raises an eyebrow. "Well, were you?"

"At first, maybe. I thought about how she seemed like someone who could fit into this life. Someone kind and genuine." I run a hand through my hair. "But I was already planning to go back to see her before you ever mentioned the marriage condition. I was drawn to her from that first day at the diner. And once I actually got to know her, once she met the family and started working here, the practical stuff stopped mattering. I fell in love with her, Uncle Harry. Really fell in love. And now she thinks it was all calculated."

"Was it?"

The question is like a slap to the face. "No. Maybe at the very beginning, but not for a long time. Not since—" I stop, trying to pinpoint the exact moment when my feelings got deeper. "Not since the night we went ice skating, and she laughed along with me when we fell. Or maybe it was when she walked through the orchard and could see the same beauty here that I do. I don't know when it happened, but it did. I planned to tell you to sell the ranch, that Patty is more important, but I didn't get that far. But I'm telling you now—I don't want the ranch anymore if Patty's not going to be happy here."

Uncle Harry nods slowly. "And you told her this?"

"I tried to. She said she needed time to think." I take another gulp of coffee. "She's still coming to the ranch today to work with Margaret, but only for Margaret's sake. Not for me."

"That's something."

"Is it? Or is she just being polite while she figures out how to let me down easy?"

Uncle Harry sets his mug on the windowsill and leans forward. "Can I tell you a story about your Aunt Margaret?"

I nod, grateful for any distraction from my spiraling thoughts.

"When Margaret and I were figuring out our feelings for each other, it took time. We'd been friends for so long, working side by side, and somewhere along the way that friendship deepened into more." Uncle Harry's expression grows thoughtful. "But we were both afraid to acknowledge it at first. Afraid of ruining what we had, afraid of being vulnerable again."

"What made you finally tell her how you felt?"

"We both realized we were being cowards. That the risk of losing each other by staying silent was greater than the risk of being honest." He takes a sip of his coffee. "The point is, real feelings don't disappear overnight, even when they're complicated by circumstances. If what you and Patty have is genuine, it'll survive this bump in the road."

"How can you be sure?"

"Because I've watched you two together. I've seen how she looks at you, and how you light up when she walks into a room." Uncle Harry's voice is gentle but firm. "That kind of connection doesn't just vanish because of poor timing or difficult conversations."

I consider this. It's reassuring to hear, though any time without her by my side feels like an eternity.

"What if she decides she can't trust me again?"

Uncle Harry's expression grows serious. "Then you accept that decision and learn from it. But Finn, if there's one thing I've learned about love, it's that it's not about perfect timing or saying the right words at the right moment. It's about showing up, day after day, as the person you really are. If your feelings for Patty are genuine, that will show through to her eventually."

"And if it doesn't?"

"Then at least you'll know you tried to do right by her." Uncle Harry stands and picks up his mug. "Give her space, son. Let her see who you are through your actions, not your words. Trust has to be earned back slowly."

After he leaves, I sit in the growing morning light thinking about his advice. Give her space. Let my actions speak for themselves.

The problem is, every instinct I have is screaming at me to go to her, to keep talking until I can make her understand. But that's exactly what Uncle Harry is warning me against. Desperation never won anyone's heart.

I spend the morning throwing myself into work with more intensity than usual. The physical labor helps quiet the churning in my mind, and by lunch I'd picked three full bins of Gala apples and helped repair a ladder that broke under one of the crew members. The repetitive motion of reaching, twisting, and dropping apples into my bag is meditative for me, and the focus helps the time pass quickly.

Of course, my focus doesn't mean much to Clarabelle.

Early afternoon I catch her sneaking into the orchard like a four-legged outlaw on a mission. Alec swears the fence was latched, but there she is, ambling between rows, nosing at apple bins and looking far too pleased with herself. I wave her off, but she ignores me like royalty brushing off the help.

"Your Duchess is back," Miguel calls out as she knocks over a half-full crate with her shoulder.

"She's not my Duchess," I mutter, jogging over to steer her toward the gate. "She just lives here rent-free and causes chaos."

Clarabelle snorts as if in agreement, then plucks a Gala straight from my open picking bag before trotting off in no particular hurry.

I glance back toward the house where I can see Patty's car parked in the drive. She arrived around eleven. I heard her car pulling down the gravel drive, but I've managed to keep my distance. Every instinct screams at me to go to the house, to check on how she's doing, to try one more time to explain. But Uncle Harry's words replay in my mind reminding me to give her space.

Alec finds me up on a ladder in the furthest row of the orchard, attacking a particularly heavy-laden tree with single-minded determination.

"Sorry about what happened at the festival," he says, settling on an overturned bucket nearby.

I don't look away from the branch I'm currently clearing. "It's fine. It was bound to come out. I should have been honest from the start."

"You're attacking that poor tree like it personally offended you."

I finally pause. "You saw how she reacted when she found out about the agreement. Now, she doesn't want anything to do with me."

"Can't say I blame her." Alec's tone is matter-of-fact. "That's a big thing to keep someone."

"I know that now."

"Question is, what are you going to do about it?"

I shrug. "What can I do? She asked for time to think. I'm giving her time to think."

"And that's killing you."

"Yeah, it's killing me." I climb down the ladder, and lean against the tree. "I love her, Alec. Really love her. And I might have screwed it up beyond repair because I was too much of a coward to be honest from the start."

Alec's quiet for a moment, studying my face. "You know what I think?"

"What?"

"I think if you really love her, you'll find a way to prove it. Show her that she matters more than the ranch, more than anything else."

"How do I do that?"

"I don't know. But you're a smart guy. You'll figure it out."

The afternoon brings a steady stream of harvest work, but my mind keeps drifting to the house where I know Patty's working with Margaret. I can picture her learning to mix pie crust, laughing at something

Margaret says, fitting seamlessly into the rhythm of the kitchen like she belongs there. The thought of her being so close while everything between us feels broken is almost unbearable.

But I'm determined to follow Uncle Harry's advice, and give her the space she asked for.

Because if there's any chance of earning back her trust, it starts with showing her that I can put her needs before my own. That I can love her enough to give her space, even if it means I risk losing her.

The ranch has been in my family for generations, but Patty . . . Patty is my future. And she's worth fighting for.

I just hope I'm strong enough to keep waiting as long as she needs me to.

CHAPTER FIFTEEN

Patty

I sit in my car outside the farmhouse for a full minute before turning off the engine, trying to settle my nerves. Coming back to Apple Blossom Ranch after everything that happened at the festival feels strange and loaded with tension I'm not sure how to navigate.

But I made a promise to Margaret, and more importantly, I refuse to let Finn's poor timing destroy the sense of belonging I've found since leaving Klive.

Margaret appears on the porch before I've even gathered my purse, waving with a dish towel and beaming like nothing in the world has changed. The sight of her genuine happiness to see me eases some of the tightness in my chest.

"Patty! Perfect timing. I just pulled the apple turnovers out of the oven for the crew's afternoon snack."

"Morning, Margaret." I climb the porch steps, grateful for her easy warmth. "What can I help with today?"

"Well, I thought we could tackle that apple pie recipe I've been promising to teach you. We'll need about six pies for Sunday dinner, so it'll be good practice."

She doesn't mention my argument with Finn, or ask probing questions about my feelings, and it makes me want to hug her. Instead, I follow her into the kitchen and tie on the apron she hands me.

"Six pies sounds ambitious," I say, rolling up my sleeves.

"Not when you know the secret." Margaret winks and starts pulling ingredients from the pantry. "My grandmother's recipe uses a touch of cardamom in the filling. Makes all the difference."

For the next hour, we work side by side in a comfortable rhythm. Margaret walks me through her pie crust technique, teaching me how to keep the butter cold, how to know when you've mixed it just enough, and how to roll it out without overworking the dough. It's soothing work, and I find myself relaxing for the first time since I arrived.

"You're a natural at this," Margaret says, watching me crimp the edges of my first pie. "Look at those perfect little scallops."

"I had a good teacher." I step back to admire my work. "My grandmother tried to teach me when I was little, but I was too impatient. I wanted to eat the pie, not make it."

"Well, patience comes with age. And motivation." Margaret slides two pies into the oven and sets the timer. "A woman who wants to feed people she cares about will learn to make anything."

Her words hang in the air between us, gentle but pointed. I know she's not just talking about cooking.

"Margaret," I start, then stop. I'm not sure how much Finn has told her about our conversation.

"Yes, dear?"

"Did Finn tell you what happened?"

Margaret pauses in her measuring of flour, then continues with steady hands. "He mentioned you two had a difficult conversation. He also said I shouldn't pry, and that your friendship with me shouldn't be affected by whatever's happening between you two."

The fact that Finn specifically protected my relationship with Margaret makes warmth unfurl in my chest.

"I found out about Uncle Harry's condition," I say quietly. "That Finn needs to be married."

"Ah." Margaret nods slowly. "That explains the long face he's been wearing. And why he's been working the farthest section of the orchard all morning."

"He's avoiding me."

"He's respecting your space. There's a difference." Margaret meets my eyes directly. "That boy could have found a dozen excuses to come to the house today. Check on lunch prep, grab a tool from the shed, ask me a question about the harvest schedule. Instead, he's staying away because he thinks that's what you need."

She's right. The Finn from a week ago would have found reasons to be near me, to steal moments of conversation or touch my hand when passing me something. Today, I haven't seen him once.

"I do need some time. I miss him, but I have to figure out how I feel now that I know his reasons . . ." I say, more to myself than to Margaret.

"Only you can answer that." Margaret starts mixing the filling for the next batch of pies. "But I will say this. I've watched a lot of people fall in love over the years—I did it twice, myself—and I've learned to recognize the difference between someone who loves the idea of you and someone who loves you."

"What's the difference?"

"Someone who loves the *idea* of you wants you to fit into their life exactly as they've imagined it. Someone who loves *you* is willing to change their life to make room for who you really are." Margaret adds a pinch of cardamom to the cinnamon and sugar mixture. "Which one do you think Finn is?"

I think about this as we work. Finn never tried to change me or make me smaller. He encouraged my friendship with Margaret, supported my work at the diner, celebrated my small victories like learning to ice skate or mastering Margaret's cornbread recipe.

He was willing to give up the ranch for me.

"I think he loves me," I admit quietly. "The real me. I'm just scared that the timing of everything means his feelings got tangled up with the hope of keeping the ranch."

"And what if they did?" Margaret asks gently. "What if he realized he cared about you and then thought, 'What luck, she could also be part of this life I'm building'? Would that make his feelings less real?"

"I . . . I don't know."

"Love isn't always convenient, honey. Sometimes it shows up at complicated times, mixed up with other parts of our lives."

Margaret's words make me think. Maybe the timing doesn't matter as much as I thought it did. Maybe what matters is how Finn treats me, how genuine his feelings seem when we're together.

We work in comfortable silence for a while, the kitchen filling with the warm scent of baking apples and cinnamon. Through the window, I can see the crew working in the near orchard, but no sign of Finn. Margaret was right. He really is staying away.

"Margaret," I say as we start rolling out dough for the fourth pie. "Can I ask you a personal question?"

"Of course."

"When you and Harry were figuring out your feelings for each other, were you ever scared it was too good to be true?"

Margaret's hands go still on the rolling pin. "Every day," she says softly. "After Fred died, I convinced myself I was done with love. That I'd had my chance and it would be greedy to ask for another one. When Harry started looking at me differently, started making excuses to spend time with me, I was terrified."

"What changed?"

"I realized I was so busy protecting myself from getting hurt that I was guaranteeing I'd never be happy again." Margaret looks at me directly. "Love is always a risk, honey. The question is whether the person is worth it."

Before I can respond, the back door opens and Alec walks in, dusty from the orchard and grinning when he sees the pies cooling on the counter.

"Please tell me one of those is for taste-testing," he says, washing his hands at the sink.

"They're for Sunday dinner," Margaret says firmly. "But I might have a turnover left from this morning's batch."

"You're a saint." Alec accepts the pastry gratefully, then glances at me. "Good to see you here, Patty."

"Thank you." I feel heat rise in my cheeks. "It's good to be here."

Alec takes a bite of the turnover and groans appreciatively. "This is incredible. Finn's been missing out, working clear on the other side of the property all day."

"He's giving me space," I say quietly.

"Yeah, well, he's being so respectful it's driving him crazy." Alec's tone is gentle and honest. "I've never seen a man pick apples so . . . aggressively."

I almost giggle at the image. "Aggressive apple picking?"

"Three bins before lunch. Miguel thinks he's trying to set some kind of record." Alec finishes his turnover and heads for the door. "Just thought you should know. Whatever you're thinking, he's not staying away because he doesn't want to see you. He'd be here in a heartbeat if you wanted him to."

After Alec leaves, Margaret and I finish the last two pies in silence. I find myself glancing out the window more often, half hoping to catch a glimpse of Finn, half relieved when I don't.

By the time we're cleaning up from our baking marathon, the afternoon sun is starting to slant low through the kitchen windows. Six perfect pies cool on the counter, and I feel a deep satisfaction at having learned something new.

"Thank you for the lesson," I tell Margaret as I untie my apron.

"Thank you for not letting whatever's happening between you and Finn keep you away from here." Margaret gives me a motherly hug. "You belong here, Patty. Whatever else happens, don't forget that."

As I walk to my car, I find myself scanning the orchard for any sign of Finn. I don't see him, but somehow I can feel his presence. The fact that he's stayed away all day when I know he must be dying to talk to me means a lot.

Halfway across the gravel drive, movement catches my eye near the edge of the orchard. Clarabelle ambles between the trees like she owns the place. She pauses to stare at me, then flicks her tail and continues on her way, as if I've passed some sort of bovine inspection. If only judging someone's character was that easy for me.

I think Margaret's right. If someone truly loves you—not just the idea of you—he shows you through his actions, even when those actions require sacrifice.

The question is whether I'm brave enough to find out which one Finn really is.

I drive home thinking about cardamom and pie crust and the difference between love and the idea of love. For the first time since Monday night, the tight knot in my chest has loosened slightly.

It's not forgiveness. But it might be the beginning of understanding.

CHAPTER SIXTEEN

Finn

I'm replacing a broken rung on one of the orchard ladders Sunday morning when I hear the gravel crunch of Patty's car pulling into the drive. My hands still on the wood, and I have to force myself not to look toward the house. She came back again. After four days of wondering how she's been, I'm glad to know she's okay. Or at least okay enough to come back.

"You planning to sand that rung down to nothing?" Miguel asks, settling beside me with his own repair project.

"Just want to make sure it's smooth," I mutter, though I realize I've been rubbing the same spot with sandpaper for the past ten minutes.

"Uh-huh." Miguel's tone is knowing. "And this wouldn't have anything to do with the pretty lady who just arrived?"

I set down the sandpaper and reach for the wood stain. "She needs some time away from me, so I'm giving it to her."

"That's good. But you look like a man who's about to crawl out of his skin."

He's not wrong. It's been six days since our conversation at the festival, and every minute feels like an hour. Wednesday went well from what I heard. She worked with Margaret, seemed comfortable, even asked about me, according to Alec. But four days is a long time to wonder if she's been thinking about us or trying to forget about us.

"She asked for time to think," I say, fitting the new rung into place. "I'm respecting that. Even if it kills me."

"And what happens if she decides she needs more time than you have?"

"Then I wait. She's worth it."

Miguel nods approvingly. "Good man. The right woman's worth more than any piece of land."

The past few days have been a study in patience I never knew I had. Thursday, I drove to town early and fixed the loose lock on the diner's back door. I'd noticed it weeks ago but never got around to addressing it. Ms. Daisy caught me finishing up and gave me one of her knowing looks, but I pretended it was just neighborly maintenance.

Friday, I helped Ruth, Patty's landlord, with some loose gutters on her garage. She'd mentioned at the feed store that they were rattling in the wind, keeping her awake. Again, just being helpful. The fact that it might make Patty's living situation a little more peaceful was just a bonus.

Saturday, I resisted the urge to drive by Beats and Eats three separate times.

By noon today, I've repaired two more ladders and helped Miguel fix a broken wheel on one of the harvest bins. The physical work helps, but my awareness of Patty's presence in the house hums under everything like a live wire.

When Alec heads in for lunch, I volunteer to stay in the orchard and keep working. The last thing I want is to run into Patty in the kitchen and make her uncomfortable. She needs to know she can be here without worrying about me bothering her.

Twenty minutes later, Alec returns with a sandwich and a look I can't quite read.

"She asked where you were again," he says without preamble.

My heart does a complicated flip in my chest. Like a somersault, but more uncoordinated. "What did you tell her?"

"Same thing as Wednesday." Alec unwraps his sandwich and takes a bite. "I think she might be ready for a little less space."

"What do you mean?"

"She seemed disappointed that you're still working the far sections. And she mentioned the lock at the diner. Said it was thoughtful." Alec studies my face. "I think your middle-ground approach is working."

Relief washes through me, followed immediately by hope. "She mentioned the lock?"

"And the fact that Ruth's gutters stopped rattling Friday night." Alec's grin is knowing. "Word gets around when someone's taking care of people."

I hadn't realized Patty would connect those dots, but I should've known better. Piney Brook's too small for anonymous good deeds.

"What would you do?" I ask. "If you were me?"

"Me? I'd probably mess it up completely." Alec grins. "But if I were smart, I'd maybe find a reason to work closer to the house. Not to bother her, just to let her see you're still here if she wants to talk."

"That doesn't sound like giving her space."

"It's been six days, Finn. Sometimes space turns into distance if you're not careful. Trust me."

The afternoon drags on, but Alec's words stick with me. By three o'clock, I find myself working the orchard section closest to the house instead of the far rows where I've been hiding out all week. It's a compromise. I'm close enough that she might see me if she looks out the kitchen window, but not so close that I'm obviously hovering.

I position myself behind a ladder, pretending to check the irrigation lines, but really just hoping for a glimpse of her through the farmhouse windows. Like a lovesick teenager. The thought would be embarrassing if I weren't so desperate for any sign that she's okay.

When I catch sight of her moving around the kitchen, my chest tightens with relief and longing. She's wearing the blue sweater that brings out her eyes, her hair pulled back in the ponytail she favors when she's working. Even from this distance, she looks beautiful. She looks like home.

I watch as she and Margaret work side by side, probably preparing tomorrow's bread or some desserts. Seeing Patty in that kitchen makes the ache in my chest even worse. I love imagining her by my side on our own ranch someday, but if she wanted me to join the circus instead, I'd do it for her. We belong together. I just have to figure out how to prove that to her.

When she moves to the window above the sink I duck behind the apple tree like a guilty fool. But not before I see her pause, looking out toward the orchard. Looking for me, maybe? Or just checking on the day's progress? I can't tell from this distance, but the possibility that she might be thinking about me makes me smile.

I spend the rest of the afternoon finding reasons to work within sight of the house, always careful to look busy, never lingering too long in one spot. It's a delicate balance, being present without being pushy, showing her I'm here without making her feel pressured to acknowledge it.

When I see her car pull away around five, the familiar hollow feeling settles in my chest. Another day of loving her from a distance. Another evening of wondering if I've lost her forever.

That evening, after the crew has headed to the bunkhouse, I make my way to the kitchen. Margaret's cleaning up from dinner prep, humming softly to herself.

"How did it go today?" I ask, settling at the counter.

"Good. She's a quick learner, and those hands were made for pastry work." Margaret glances at me sideways. "She asked about you."

My pulse quickens. "What kind of asking?"

"The concerned kind. She noticed you stayed away all day again." Margaret sets down her dish towel and turns to face me fully. "Finn, there's a difference between respecting someone's space and disappearing completely."

"That's what Alec said."

"Then maybe you should listen to Alec." Margaret's tone is gentle but firm. "That girl cares about you. She's hurt and confused, but she cares. Don't make her think you've given up."

"I don't want to pressure her."

"Then don't. You can be around without pressuring her."

That night, I lie awake thinking about the difference between patience and absence, and devise a plan.

I'm up before dawn, same as always, but instead of heading straight to the orchard, I detour and find myself in the workshop behind the barn, surrounded by wood shavings and the smell of apple wood. I decided to make her something she'll find useful, but will show that I care about her. I remembered how excited Patty gets when Margaret teaches her a new recipe, how she carefully writes down every instruction, so I'm making her a recipe box out of wood salvaged from an old apple tree we had to remove after a storm.

The box isn't fancy when I'm finished. I don't have fine woodworking skills for detailed carving, but it's solid and smooth, and made to last.

Just as I'm wiping it down, the workshop door creaks open and Clarabelle wanders in like she owns the place.

"Don't even think about chewing the workbench," I mutter, pointing a finger in her direction.

She snorts and plops down like some oversized dog, her head resting dramatically on the floor with a sigh that makes me laugh under my breath.

"You know," I say, glancing at her, "for a cow, you've got surprisingly good timing."

She flicks her tail in response, but doesn't move, content to keep me company while I polish the box one last time.

Before heading to the orchard, I drive into town. Beats and Eats won't open for another hour, but I know Ms. Daisy arrives early for prep work. I park behind the diner and carry the small box to the back door.

"Finn Miller," Ms. Daisy says when she answers my knock. "You're up early."

"Morning, Ms. Daisy. I have a gift for Patty, but I don't want to make a big deal of it." I hold out the box. "Could you give this to her when she comes in?"

Ms. Daisy takes the package, weighing it in her hands with curiosity. "This wouldn't happen to be handmade, would it?"

Heat creeps up my neck. "Just thought she might have a use for it."

"Mm-hmm." Ms. Daisy's smile is knowing. "Well, whatever it is, I'm sure she'll appreciate the thought. That girl's been through enough worry in her life. Nice to know there are people looking out for her."

I head back to the ranch feeling lighter than I have in days. It's a small gesture, but it feels right. A gift, made with my own hands, that says I see her, I notice what matters to her.

I don't know what will happen next. I don't know if she'll ever fully trust me again, or if we'll figure out a way forward together. But at least this shows her that I care about her—not about saving the ranch or meeting a deadline. I care about the woman who gets excited learning new recipes, who writes down every instruction with careful precision, who's building a new life one small piece at a time.

Maybe it's enough for now to rebuild her trust one small, honest gesture at a time.

CHAPTER SEVENTEEN

Patty

The recipe box sits on my kitchen counter, right next to my grand-mother's old recipe book. I've been staring at it for ten minutes, running my fingers over the smooth wood.

When Ms. Daisy handed it to me yesterday morning with that know-ing smile of hers, I knew immediately who it was from. The craftsman-ship, the thoughtfulness, it could only be Finn. No one has ever made me a present like this before, and it makes me feel seen.

Klive used to buy me expensive jewelry for birthdays and holi-days—flashy pieces that looked impressive but never felt like me. They were gifts that said "look what I can afford" rather than "I see who you are." This simple wooden box says everything those diamonds never could.

My phone buzzes on the counter. A text from Anne.

Anne: *Coffee this morning? I'm dying to hear about your week.*

I glance at the clock. I have an hour before my shift starts.

Me: *Meet you at the diner in 20?*

Anne: *Perfect. Can't wait to see this mysterious gift you mentioned.*

I grab my purse and the recipe box—the one made especially for me. As I lock my apartment door, I catch myself humming, something I haven't done in years. The morning air is crisp with the promise of a cold snap coming, and I pull my jacket tighter as I walk to the car.

The drive to the diner passes in a blur of autumn colors. I'm content, I realize. Everything about my life in Piney Brook feels too good to be true sometimes. The job I love, friends who care about me, a man who made me a wooden recipe box because he notices I collect recipes. It's the kind of life I thought only existed in movies.

When I arrive at the diner a few minutes later, Anne's already waiting at the counter, practically vibrating with curiosity.

"Is that it?" she asks before I've even said hello.

I set the box carefully on the counter between us. "He made it himself."

Anne runs her fingers gently over the wood. "Patty, this is beautiful."

"I know." I lift the lid to show her the inside, fitted with small dividers perfect for index cards. "It's exactly what I need for all the recipes Margaret's been teaching me."

"This isn't just thoughtful," Anne says, studying my face. "This is. . . this is love, honey. The real kind. The kind that pays attention to what matters to you."

Heat rises in my cheeks. "It's just a wooden box."

Anne's smile is knowing. "This man spent hours making this for you, Patty. To me that shows that you're special to him, and that he really knows you."

"That's what scares me," I admit quietly. "It's been so long since someone saw me like that. Sometimes I worry I'm reading too much into things, you know? Making it bigger than it is because I want it so badly."

"Honey," Anne says, closing the lid of the box and pushing it slightly toward me, "you're not imagining this. Trust yourself. Trust your instincts. They brought you here, didn't they? Away from whatever you were running from?"

The mention of running makes dread settle in my stomach, but I push it away. That's the past. This is my life now. I won't run again.

Before I can respond, the bell above the door chimes. I look up expecting to see an early customer, but my blood turns to ice when I see who's walking in.

Klive.

He looks exactly the same—sandy brown hair, smug expression—I don't know what I ever saw in him. He has his usual calculating look in his pale blue eyes, and he's scanning the room like he's assessing threats and opportunities.

"Patty?" Anne's voice sounds far away. "Honey, you've gone white as a sheet."

I can't speak. Can't move. Can't do anything but watch as Klive spots me and starts walking over with that familiar, predatory smile.

"Patricia," he says, his voice warm and friendly for Anne's benefit. "You look wonderful. Small-town life must agree with you."

I find my voice, though it comes out smaller than I'd like. "What are you doing here, Klive?"

"I came to see you, of course." He settles onto the stool next to Anne like he belongs here, like he has every right to invade the safe space I've built. "I've missed you."

Anne looks between us, clearly trying to piece together what's happening. I see the moment she figures it out. Her expression hardens and she shifts slightly, putting herself between Klive and me.

"I'm Anne," she says sweetly. "I don't think we've met."

"Klive Fritz," he says, extending his hand with that charming smile that used to fool everyone. "Patty's husband."

"Ex-husband," I correct quickly. "We're divorced."

"A mistake I'm hoping to remedy," Klive says, his eyes never leaving my face. "I've done a lot of thinking since you left, Patricia. A lot of growing. I realize now how I failed you as a husband."

The practiced words, the humble tone . . . It's all part of the act. The same performance he gave the marriage counselor, the pastor, anyone who might have helped me if they'd known the truth.

"I need to get ready for my shift," I say, standing on shaky legs.

"Of course. You're working now. I'm proud of you for that." Klive's smile doesn't waver. "I'm staying at the motel just outside town. Maybe we could have dinner tonight? Talk about things?"

"No." The word comes out more firmly than I expected. "I don't want to have dinner with you, Klive. I don't want to talk about things. I want you to leave."

Anger flickers in his eyes—just for a second—before the pleasant mask slides back into place. "I understand you're angry. You have every right to be. But I've changed, Patricia. I'm in therapy now. I've learned so much about myself, about how I hurt you."

The reasonable tone, the mention of therapy, the acknowledgment of fault. It's all calculated to make me seem unreasonable if I don't give him a chance. He hasn't changed. Not one bit.

"That's good for you," I manage. "But it doesn't change anything between us."

"Doesn't it?" He leans forward slightly, and I have to force myself not to step back. "We had something special once, Patricia. We can have it again. I know we can. You know I never signed those divorce papers. As far as I'm concerned, we're still married. We belong together."

"Her name is Patty," Anne says firmly. "And she asked you to leave."

Klive glances at Anne with the kind of dismissive look he used to give anyone who tried to interfere. "This is between my wife and me."

"Ex-wife," Anne corrects. "And she's my friend. If she wants you gone, you need to go."

The tension in the air is thick enough to cut. I can see other early customers starting to notice, and the last thing I want is to make a scene. That's what Klive's counting on, though. My desire to avoid confrontation, to keep things peaceful.

"I'll go," Klive says, standing up with the air of a martyr. "But I'm not giving up on us, Patricia. I love you. I always have."

He reaches for my hand, and this time I do step back.

"Don't," I say, surprised by the steadiness in my voice. "Don't touch me. Not ever again."

His mask slips again, and I see the flash of anger before he covers it. "I'll be in town for a few days. In case you change your mind."

After he leaves, I sink back onto my stool, my hands shaking so badly I can barely hold my coffee cup.

"That's the one who hurt you," Anne says. It's not a question.

I nod, not trusting my voice.

Anne reaches over and covers my trembling hand with hers. "You were amazing just now. Do you see how strong you are? You told him no. You set boundaries. You didn't let him manipulate you."

"I don't feel strong. I feel scared."

"Yeah, well . . . Sometimes being strong means being scared and pushing through, anyway." Anne squeezes my hand. "Are you going to be okay to work today?"

I think about hiding in my apartment versus staying in public, surrounded by people who care about me. About letting Klive disrupt my life versus continuing in the routine that's given me stability.

"Yes," I say, and mean it. "I'm going to work. I'm not letting him chase me away from my life."

Anne grins. "That's my girl. You're stronger than you give yourself credit for. And Patty? You might want to let certain people know he's in town. People who care about you and might want to keep an eye out."

She doesn't say Finn's name, but we both know who she means.

I look down at the recipe box, at the evidence of someone who sees me and values me for who I am. Then I look toward the door where Klive disappeared, the man who only ever saw me as property to own and control.

The contrast is so stark it takes my breath away.

For the first time since last Monday night, I know exactly what I want to do.

I want to fight for this life I've built. I want to protect the happiness I've found. And I want to trust that the people who care about me will help me do it.

I'm not the same woman who left Tennessee in the middle of the night. I'm stronger now. And I'm not going down without a fight.

CHAPTER EIGHTEEN

Finn

I'm loading the last of the morning's apple harvest into the truck when Alec jogs over from the direction of the house, a troubled look on his face.

"Finn," he says, slightly out of breath. "Margaret just got a call from Ms. Daisy."

My stomach immediately tightens. "What kind of call?"

"Patty's ex-husband showed up at the diner this morning. Made a scene, trying to get her to talk to him. Ms. Daisy wanted Margaret to know in case . . ." He trails off, but I understand the implication.

The apple I'm holding drops from my hand. My fingers go numb, and suddenly I can't seem to get enough air. The rational part of my brain knows Patty's safe at work—Ms. Daisy's as good as a bouncer, if it came to that—but every protective instinct I have is screaming.

"Is she okay?"

"According to Ms. Daisy, she handled it like a champ. Told him to leave and meant it. But the guy's staying at the Motor Inn out on the west highway, and says he's not giving up."

Rage builds in my chest, hot and fast, followed immediately by a helpless feeling that makes my hands shake. I clench them into fists, trying to regain control. The man who hurt Patty, who made her afraid to trust again, is here. In our town. And there's nothing I can do about it without making things worse for her.

"I have to go to her," I say, already heading for my truck.

"Finn, wait." Alec catches my arm. "Think about this. She's at work. She's safe there. And if you go charging in there like some kind of white knight, you might make her feel like you don't trust her to handle her own problems."

The words stop me in my tracks. He's right. As much as every instinct screams at me to get to Patty, to stand between her and any threat, that's not what she needs from me. She needs to know I believe in her.

"But I can't just do nothing," I say, running a hand through my hair.

"You're not doing nothing. You're respecting her independence, but you're ready if she needs you." Alec's voice is calm, reasonable. "Send her a text—keep it short and sweet—and leave the ball in her court."

I pull out my phone with trembling fingers, typing and deleting the same message three times before finally sending a simple message.

Me: *I'm thinking of you.*

I hit send and immediately want to type more. *Are you okay? Do you need me? Should I come?* But I force myself to put the phone away.

The rest of the morning passes in a haze of distraction. I drop too many apples, nearly fall off a ladder when my mind wanders, and accidentally dump a full bin of Honeycrisps because I'm not paying attention to what I'm doing.

"Hermano," Miguel says, appearing at my elbow around eleven, "you're going to hurt yourself if you keep working like this."

I pause, realizing I've been staring at the same apple for the past five minutes. "Sorry. I'm fine."

"No, you're not." Miguel studies my face. "What's going on?"

I glance around, making sure we're out of earshot of the other crew members. "Patty's ex-husband is in town. He showed up at the diner this morning."

Miguel's expression darkens immediately. "He came to find her?"

"Yeah."

"And you're out here picking apples instead of—" Miguel stops himself, shaking his head. "No, I get it. She's a big girl. I'm sure she can manage him, and you being there might make things worse."

"That's what Alec said."

"Alec's right. But that doesn't make it easier." Miguel puts a hand on my shoulder. "My sister went through a similar situation. The hardest part was staying back and letting her be strong."

"What if he hurts her?"

"If that happens, we'll deal with him. But, Finn, don't sell her short. She survived him once. She can do it again."

I spend the rest of the morning working with half my attention on the apple trees and half on my phone, waiting for a reply that doesn't come. By lunch, I'm wound tighter than a spring, imagining worst-case scenarios and fighting the urge to drive into town just to lay eyes on her.

When Margaret appears with sandwiches for the crew, I pull her aside.

"Any word from Ms. Daisy?"

"She called again around ten. Said Patty's working her shift like nothing happened, but she's keeping an eye on things." Margaret's expression is concerned but admiring. "Don't worry too much. That girl's strong."

"I know she is. I just hate that she has to be."

"Sometimes the people we love face battles we can't fight for them," Margaret says gently. "The best we can do is make sure they know we're in their corner."

Around two o'clock, I'm working in the orchard closest to the road when I hear a car pull into the ranch drive. My heart jumps, hoping it's Patty, but when I look toward the house, I see an unfamiliar sedan. A man gets out. He's average height, with light brown hair, the kind of unremarkable face that would help him blend in anywhere.

Seeing him makes my hackles rise, and I get a strong feeling this is Patty's ex-husband. My blood turns to ice, and every muscle in my body tenses.

Just as I'm stepping out from under the trees to get a better look, a familiar snort drifts from my right.

Clarabelle.

The Duchess herself is standing beside the cooler Margaret set out for the crew, eyeing the giant container of sweet tea like it's her personal treat. Before I can stop her, she noses the cooler hard, sending it toppling to the ground and causing the lid to pop off. Gallons of sweet tea pour into the grass and splash onto her hooves.

Clarabelle lets out a happy huff and laps at the spilled tea, flicking her tail in delight.

"Of course you'd choose now to make a mess," I mutter under my breath, grabbing the cooler and lid and putting it back up on the table. "You're a real pain, you know that?"

Clarabelle lets out an indignant *moo*, flicks her tail, and ambles away toward the far pasture.

Small mercies.

I turn my attention back to the creeper at our door. Every instinct tells me to march over there, to get between this man and my family, but Alec's words echo in my head. The last thing Patty needs is for me to make this worse.

I watch, arms folded, as Margaret opens the door and, even from this distance, I can see the set of her shoulders, and how she positions herself in the doorway without inviting him in.

I'm too far away to hear the conversation, but I can see her shake her head firmly several times. After a few minutes, the man gets back in his car and drives away, but not before glancing toward the orchard where I'm standing.

The look he gives in my direction sends a chill down my spine. It's calculating, assessing. Like he's filing away information for later use.

I make my way to the house, my jaw clenched tight.

"Was that him?" I ask Margaret.

"Klive Fritz," she confirms, her voice clipped with distaste. "Said he was looking for Patty, that he heard she worked here. I told him she wasn't on the property and that he wasn't welcome. He knew good and well she wasn't here today."

"What else did he say?"

"He wanted me to give her a message—that he's staying in town until she agrees to see him." Margaret's expression hardens.

"And he just left?"

"After I made it clear he wouldn't be getting any information from me." Margaret glances toward the orchard where I've been working. "He asked if Patty had a boyfriend."

"What did you tell him?"

"That her personal life was none of his business." Margaret puts a hand on my arm. "You did the right thing, staying back. Men like that are always looking for someone to blame, someone to focus their anger on. The last thing Patty needs is for him to see you as a rival and escalate things. I'll be glad to sic you and Harry and the whole crew on him if he comes back, though."

The thought of this man focusing his attention on me doesn't scare me, but the idea of him hurting Patty because of me makes my stomach turn.

"Should I stay away from her completely until he leaves?"

"I don't know," Margaret admits. "I think we should let Patty decide what she needs."

Back in the orchard, I try to return to work, but my hands won't stop shaking. Every time a car passes on the road, I look up, half expecting to see that sedan again.

"Boss," Sara says during the afternoon water break, "maybe you should call it a day. You're wound tighter than a two-dollar watch."

"I'm fine," I insist, but even I can hear how unconvincing it sounds.

"No, you're not," Miguel says bluntly. "And that's okay. When someone you love is in danger, 'fine' isn't an option."

That evening, I pace the front porch like a caged animal, my phone in my hand. I've typed and deleted a dozen texts to Patty, unsure what to say.

Me: *I'm here if you need me.*

Her response comes twenty minutes later.

Patty: *Thank you. That means a lot.*

It's not much, but the fact that she responded at all eases some of the tension I've been carrying. She's okay. She's got this. And she knows she can count on me.

Uncle Harry finds me on the porch around sunset, two iced teas in his hands.

"Margaret told me what happened," he says, passing me a glass, then settles into the chair beside mine.

"Yeah, this whole thing stinks. I keep seeing that guy's stupid face in my head and I'm forced to sit here and do nothing."

"No, you're being patient and trusting a very smart woman." Uncle Harry takes a sip of his iced tea. "She'll be all right. It takes some kind of mettle to leave what she left. If she did that, she's going to be fine."

As the stars come out above the orchard, I think about Uncle Harry's words. He's right. That woman's got mettle. And so much more. I picture her blushing that first day I called her "sugar." That grin of hers. And I think of her surrounded by her circle of friends, and how hardworking she is. She gets a vision of what she wants, and she jumps in with both feet. She's amazing. I am so lucky to have any part in her life.

She's also the woman who called me out when I wasn't being honest with her, who demanded better from me and from our relationship. If she could stand up to me when I was wrong, she can definitely handle Klive.

She doesn't need me to rescue her. She needs me to trust her.

CHAPTER NINETEEN

Patty

My hands shake slightly as I tie my apron Tuesday morning, but I force myself to focus on the familiar routine. Coffee brewing, tables wiped down, sugar dispensers filled. Normal tasks that ground me in the life I've built here.

When the bell above the door chimes, my shoulders tense. But it's just Mrs. Peterson wanting her usual scrambled eggs, then Jim from the hardware store grabbing coffee to go, then a traveling salesman I don't recognize who orders pancakes and keeps to himself.

"You doing okay, honey?" Ms. Daisy asks during a lull between breakfast and lunch. "You seem jumpy."

"Just tired," I lie, not wanting to worry her more than I already have. I am tired, though. My body jolted me awake every time I dozed off last night.

She gives me a knowing look but doesn't push. "Well, if you need anything, you just holler."

The lunch rush keeps me busy enough that I almost forget to be nervous. Almost. But when Anne stops by for her usual Tuesday sandwich, I find myself scanning the parking lot through the window before sitting down with her.

"He hasn't come back?" Anne asks, following my gaze.

"Not yet. But I keep expecting him to." I refill her coffee cup with hands that are steadier than they were this morning. "I hate that he's in my head like this."

"It's normal to be on edge. You stood up to him yesterday. That was huge. But that doesn't mean you stop being careful."

I nod, grateful for her understanding. "The weird thing is, I keep thinking Finn's going to show up. Like, dramatically burst through the door to check on me."

"He hasn't?"

"No. He texted a couple times yesterday, and that's it." I pause, realizing what that means. "There's no way he hasn't heard about Klive being in town. He must be waiting for me to *ask* him for help."

"And how does that feel?"

I consider the question as I watch a family with young kids settle into their booth, the parents looking frazzled but happy. "Good," I say, surprised by the truth of it. "It feels like he trusts me."

"That's because he does."

"Klive never trusted me with anything. He had opinions on what I wore, who I talked to, how I spent my time." I shake my head. "Finn's not like that."

"Finn's not Klive."

"No," I agree. "He's really not."

The afternoon passes more quietly. I serve coffee to the book club ladies, take a pie order from Mrs. Henderson, and help Ms. Daisy prep vegetables for tomorrow's soup. Normal Tuesday things that remind me this is my life now.

But when my shift ends and I walk toward the parking lot, my calm evaporates. There he is, leaning against my car like he owns it, like he has every right to be there waiting for me. My steps falter for just a moment before I force myself to keep walking.

"Hello, Patricia," he says, straightening up as I approach. "I was hoping we could talk."

"I told you yesterday I don't want to talk to you." I stop a few feet away, my keys ready in my hand. "Please move away from my car."

"Just five minutes," he says, not moving. "That's all I'm asking. Surely you can spare five minutes for the man you were married to for three years."

His reasonable tone, the slight guilt trip about our shared history—it's all so familiar. But instead of the old automatic compliance, I feel anger. Clear, clean anger at his presumption.

"I don't owe you five minutes. I don't owe you anything." I step closer to my car. "Move."

"I've been thinking about us, about what we had—"

"What we had was you hurting me," I interrupt, surprised by the steadiness in my own voice. "What we had was you controlling every aspect of my life until I forgot who I was."

His mask slips slightly, irritation flickering across his features. "You're being dramatic, Patricia. I made mistakes, yes, but—"

"Don't." The word comes out sharp. "Don't minimize what you did to me. Don't call it 'mistakes.' You chose to hurt me, again and again."

"I'm not that person anymore," he insists, infusing his voice with the familiar charisma that works on so many people. "I've learned how to communicate better. I've grown."

"Good for you. That still doesn't change anything between us."

"Of course it does. Listen, everyone asks about you. They all say how good you were for me. I saw that I needed to change, and I have. We had a good life before. I took care of you. Don't you miss that? We can start over, be better together—"

"There is no 'us,' Klive. There will never be an 'us' again." I take another step toward my car, forcing him to move or physically block me. "I'm not the same person either, thank goodness. And I'm not afraid of you. I don't owe you five minutes of my day. I listened to you for three years and I don't want to anymore. That's why I left you. I have a life here now, people who care about me, work that I love. I'm not going back to being your emotional punching bag. Or your literal one either."

A darkness flashes in his eyes. "So that's it? You're going to throw away three years of marriage for what? This *nothing* little town? Some dead-end waitressing job?"

"Yes," I say simply. "How's that feel, Klive? I'd rather be happy and alone in this 'nothing little town' than miserable with you anywhere. "

"Alone, huh? And what about your boyfriend?" The words come out ugly, loaded with insinuation. "The rancher you've been sleeping with. Does he know what you're really like? How needy and cold you can be when you're not playing the victim?"

The old me would have flinched at the accusation, would have tried to defend myself or deny the relationship. The new me recognizes the manipulation for what it is.

"You know nothing about him, or us," I say. "But I will tell you this—I am loved here. I have wealth far greater than you'll ever have because I have real friends. A community. And I'm building a relationship with someone who actually sees me as a person."

Klive's face hardens. "You think he's special? You think he actually cares about you? He's using you, Patricia. Just like all men use women like you."

"'Women like me?'" I laugh, and the sound surprises both of us. "You mean women who've learned to recognize manipulative abusers? Women who refuse to settle for being treated like property?"

"You're making a mistake," he says, his voice taking on the edge I remember all too well. "This fantasy life you think you've built here? It's not real. These people don't really know you. When they see who you really are—"

"Who I really am is someone who deserves better than you," I nearly shout. "Someone who deserves to be loved, not controlled. Someone strong enough to walk away from people who hurt her."

I move around him to reach my car door, and this time he doesn't try to stop me physically. But his words follow me.

"This isn't over, Patricia. I'm not giving up."

I turn back to face him one last time. "My name is Patty. And yes, this is over. It's been over since the day I left Tennessee. Now get away from my car or you might get hurt."

I get in and drive away, watching in my rearview mirror as he stands there in the parking lot, hands clenched at his sides.

My hands are shaking by the time I reach my apartment, but it's not the old fear. It's adrenaline, the aftereffects of standing up for myself like I never could when we were married. I handled him. I set boundaries and maintained them. I didn't let him twist my words or make me doubt myself.

I did that. Me.

I'm sitting on my couch, still processing what just happened, when my phone rings. Anne's name appears on the screen.

"Hey," I answer.

"Hey, yourself. How are you doing? I've been worried about you."

"I'm okay. Better than okay, actually." I tell her about the parking lot confrontation, how I stood my ground. She whoops and cheers as I tell her the details, which gives me chills and makes me smile.

"Patty, that's incredible," Anne says when I finish. "Do you hear yourself? Do you hear how strong you sound?"

"I feel strong," I admit. "For the first time in a long time, I feel like myself again."

"You are strong, girl. I'm proud of you. I'm happy for you." Anne goes quiet on the line as I think over her praise.

"Thanks. I'm happy for me too." I think about the woman who faced down her abusive ex-husband in a parking lot, about the life I've built here, and the man who made me the handmade wooden recipe box sitting on my counter.

"I know what I want," I say quietly.

"And what's that?"

"I want to stop being afraid," I say. "I want to stop letting Klive's voice in my head tell me I don't deserve good things. I'm going to trust my own judgment about people."

"Specifically about a certain rancher?"

Heat rises in my cheeks. "Yeah. Specifically about Finn."

"It's about time."

We laugh together and I think about Finn's texts from yesterday, simple and supportive. He's been giving me space to handle this situation myself instead of trying to swoop in and fix things for me. I can see now the difference between someone who trusts your strength and someone who exploits your vulnerabilities.

"I'm going to tell him how I feel," I say. "I'm going to stop punishing him for Klive's mistakes."

"Good," Anne says firmly. "Just don't let him off too easy. He did mess up, ya know."

After we hang up, I sit in the quiet of my apartment and think about the difference between the woman who left Tennessee in the middle of the night and the woman who just told her abuser exactly where he could go.

I think about Finn, probably pacing his porch and worrying about me, respecting my independence even when it must be killing him to stay away.

For the first time since the festival, I know exactly what I want to do. And tomorrow, I'm going to do it.

But tonight, I'm going to call Ms. Daisy and recommend she keep an eye out at the diner, just in case Klive decides to hurt me by wrecking the place I love. I'm not afraid of him anymore, but I'm also not stupid.

My adrenaline subsides, but I can't stop smiling as I think about a strong, handsome apple wrangler who'd give up his dream for me. I think I'll sleep just fine tonight.

CHAPTER TWENTY

Finn

I'm sitting on the front porch Wednesday evening, watching the sun set over the orchard, and it feels like it's setting on this stage of my life. It's time to start saying goodbye to this place. Uncle Harry's inside finishing up some paperwork, and when he's done I need to talk to him about finding the right buyer. He and Aunt Margaret are moving away in two and a half weeks, and it's time to make it official that I'm leaving, too.

I choose Patty, so the ranch has to go.

I should feel like I'm losing what I've always worked for. Instead, I feel peace in the hope that letting this go means I might find a way back to Patty.

My phone buzzes with a text from Margaret.

Margaret: *Patty's shift ended an hour ago. Ms. Daisy said she seemed calmer today.*

Me: *That's good. Has the ex been back to the diner?*

Margaret: *Not that I've heard. Maybe he got the message.*

I hope she's right, but I don't know if he'd give up that easily. Men who hurt women rarely accept rejection gracefully.

The sound of gravel crunching in the drive pulls me from my thoughts. I look up expecting to see Alec returning from town, but instead I see Patty's blue Honda pulling up to the house.

My heart immediately kicks into overdrive. She's here. After two days of being worried sick, I nearly sag with relief to see she's fine with my own two eyes.

I stand up as she gets out of the car, trying to read her expression in the growing twilight. She looks determined, maybe a little nervous, but not upset or scared.

"Hi," she says, walking up to the porch steps.

"Hi." I want to ask if she's okay, if she needs anything, but I force myself to wait. To let her lead this conversation.

"Is Uncle Harry around? I was hoping to talk to both of you."

My stomach drops. That sounds ominous. Like the kind of conversation that starts with "I've been thinking" and ends with goodbye.

"He's in the office. I can get him."

"Actually, can I talk to you first? Alone?"

I nod, gesturing to the chairs on the porch. She settles into the one beside mine. She looks like she's working up the courage to have a hard conversation, and somehow I know I've blown it. I've lost the best thing that's ever happened to me.

"How are you?" I ask when she doesn't immediately speak.

"I'm good. Better than good, actually." She turns to face me, and there's steel in her eyes that I haven't seen before. "Klive cornered me in the parking lot after work yesterday."

"He what?" Every muscle in my body tenses. "Are you hurt? Did he—"

"I'm fine," she says quickly. "More than fine. I handled it."

"What happened?"

She tells me everything. How he was waiting by her car, trying to manipulate her with the same old tactics. How she stood her ground, set clear boundaries, refused to let him twist her words or make her doubt herself.

"I told him it was over," she finishes. "Really over. And I meant every word."

Pride swells in my chest so fierce it takes my breath away. "You were incredible."

"I felt incredible. For the first time in years, I felt like myself again." She pauses, studying my face. "And you know what helped me realize that?"

I shake my head.

"You didn't show up at the diner. You didn't try to rescue me or fight my battles for me. You trusted me to handle it myself."

"Of course I trusted you. You're the strongest person I know. You didn't need me to step in."

"No, I didn't. But the fact that you could step back and let me be strong . . ." She takes a shaky breath. "It showed me the difference between someone who loves me and someone who wants to own me."

My heart starts pounding so hard I'm sure she can hear it. "Patty—"

"I'm not done," she says, holding up a hand. "I've been thinking about what you told me at the festival. Uncle Harry's condition, the timeline, about how your feelings for me got tangled up with everything else."

Here it comes. The rejection I've been dreading.

"I was so focused on your agreement with Harry that I missed what really mattered," she continues. "What matters isn't when you found out you needed a wife. What matters is how you treat me. How you make me feel. How you see me."

"How do you think I see you?"

"Like a person. Like someone whose thoughts and feelings actually matter." Tears glisten in her eyes. "You made me a recipe box because you noticed I like collecting Margaret's recipes. You fixed the diner's lock and Ruth's gutters without making a big deal about it. You gave me space when I asked for it, even when it must have been killing you to stay away."

"It *was* killing me," I admit.

"But you did it anyway. You let me fight my own battles. Because of that, I discovered I don't need anyone holding my hand. I'm glad I know that now." She swipes at her eyes. "I never have to worry about getting hurt again."

"Patty, what are you saying?"

She stands up, and for a terrifying moment I think she's about to leave. Instead, she moves to stand directly in front of me, close enough that I can see the gold flecks in her brown eyes.

"I'm saying that I am fine on my own, but I'd rather be with a good man who cherishes me and sacrifices his own agenda to give me what I need. Someone I can feel safe with. I'm saying I love you, Finn Miller."

The words I've been hoping to hear for weeks hit me like a physical force. "You love me?"

"I love you," she repeats, her voice stronger now. "I want to marry you. Because I can't imagine building a life with anyone else. And I want us to keep the ranch."

I stand up so fast I nearly knock over my chair. "Are you sure? Because you don't have to—"

"I'm not making this decision because I'm scared or pressured or trying to solve your problem," she interrupts. "I'm making it because facing Klive yesterday reminded me what it feels like to be with someone who doesn't truly love you. And now I know what it feels like to be with someone who does."

I cup her face in my hands, hardly believing this is real. "I do love you. More than I knew was possible."

"I know," she whispers. "I can feel it in everything you do. Can you kiss me now?"

When I kiss her, it tastes like coming home and new beginnings all at once. She melts into me, her arms wrapping around my neck, and for the first time in weeks, the knot of anxiety in my chest completely dissolves.

"So we're really doing this?" I ask when we break apart, my forehead resting against hers.

"We're really doing this." She smiles, the first smile I've seen from her since the festival. "Though I have one condition."

My stomach tightens slightly. "What's that?"

"I want us to meet Uncle Harry's deadline. Our wedding is about us choosing each other, not about saving the ranch, but—"

I interrupt her. "The ranch doesn't matter—"

"It does matter," she says firmly. "It matters to you, which means it matters to me. Also, I fell in love with you, but I'm also in love with this place. I would love to build a life here with you. It's not the reason we're getting married, but it will be a great wedding present."

I pull her closer, overwhelmed by how perfectly she understands. "Have I mentioned lately that I love you?"

"Not in the last five minutes," she teases.

"I love you, Patty Walsh. I love your strength and your kindness and how you make everything better just by being there. I love that you see the best in people and that you're brave enough to trust me again after I hurt you."

"Keep talking like that and I might marry you tomorrow."

"Don't tempt me." I grin, then grow more serious. "But first, should we tell Uncle Harry the good news? He's been worried about finding a new family to take over the ranch."

"I was hoping you'd say that." She takes my hand.

As we walk toward the house, hand in hand, I think about Uncle Harry's deadline and realize it doesn't feel like pressure anymore. It feels like a countdown to the beginning of our real life together.

"Ready?" I ask as we reach the door.

"More than ready," she says, squeezing my hand. "Let's go tell Uncle Harry he can stop worrying."

We find him in the office, bent over ledgers with his reading glasses perched on his nose. He looks up when we knock, and his face immediately brightens when he sees us together.

"Well," he says, setting down his pen. "This looks promising."

"Uncle Harry," I start, then look at Patty. "We have some news."

"Good news, I hope?"

Patty steps forward, her hand still firmly in mine. "The best news. Finn and I are getting married."

Uncle Harry's face breaks into the biggest smile I've seen from him in months. He stands up and pulls us both into a bear hug that smells like coffee and apple wood. "Margaret's going to cry," he says when he releases us. "Happy tears," he adds quickly. "The happiest tears you've ever seen."

As if summoned by her name, Margaret appears in the doorway. "I thought I heard voices—" She stops when she sees us, takes in our joined hands and glowing faces, and immediately starts tearing up.

"There's going to be another wedding," Uncle Harry announces.

"Oh, my dears," Margaret says, rushing forward to hug us both. "I'm so happy for you. When? Where? Do we need to start planning?"

"Soon," Patty says, laughing through her own tears. "I'd like to keep it simple if that's okay with Finn. Family and close friends." She turns her smiling face to me, her eyelashes sparkling with tears.

I nod. "Anything you want."

"Here at the ranch?" Margaret asks hopefully.

I look to Patty for confirmation and she nods and gives me a radiant smile. "Where else?" I say.

"Perfect," Uncle Harry says. "This calls for celebration. Margaret, do we have any of that sparkling cider left from our wedding?"

As Margaret bustles off to find cider and Uncle Harry starts talking about a guest list and the wedding dinner, I pull Patty aside.

"No regrets?" I ask quietly.

"Only that it took me so long to figure out what I wanted," she says, rising on her toes to kiss me softly. "I love you, Finn. And I can't wait to marry you."

"I love you too," I whisper against her lips. "And I promise I'll spend the rest of my life making sure you never doubt it."

Outside, the stars are coming out over the orchard where generations of my family have built their lives. But tonight, I'm not thinking about the past or family legacy.

I'm thinking about the future. Our future. And it's going to be beautiful.

CHAPTER TWENTY-ONE

Patty

Two weeks later, I'm standing in Margaret's kitchen, watching her fuss over the final details for our wedding this afternoon. I'm trying not to let the magnitude of what I'm about to do overwhelm me. In less than five hours, I'll be married to Finn. My second wedding, but this time, I know the man inside and out, and I love all of him.

"The apple turnovers are done, the rolls are rising, and the roast is marinating," Margaret says, checking items off her list. She looks up at the clock and asks, "Didn't Anne say she'd be here by eight to help with your hair?"

"Eight-thirty," I correct, smoothing down the cream satin dress hanging on the back door. "And Ms. Daisy's bringing the flowers at nine."

Margaret pauses in her list-making to study my face. "How are you feeling, sweetheart?"

"Anxious," I admit. "But like . . . happy anxious."

"That's exactly how you should feel." She sets down her pen and comes over to squeeze my hands. "You know, I've seen a lot of weddings in my time, and the best ones are the ones where both people are choosing each other with their whole hearts, and that's what you two have. You've been glowing for two weeks."

She's right. Ever since that evening on Uncle Harry's porch when everything clicked into place, I've felt lighter. Free. Like I understand the world and my place in it. When Klive showed up at the diner one last time three days ago, I didn't have to catch my breath, and my legs didn't feel weak. I told him in front of a dining room full of witnesses that if he didn't leave town immediately, I'd call the sheriff. He spluttered and fumed as he backed away from me. When the door shut behind him, Ms. Daisy and every customer in the place gave me a round of applause. I laughed and took a bow. It'll be a story I tell my kids one day.

I'm done being afraid. I'm done letting other people's opinions of me matter more than my own.

"Where's the groom?" Margaret asks with a knowing smile.

"Probably pacing the barn with Uncle Harry, wondering if it's too late to elope." I laugh. "He's been a nervous wreck all week."

"Good. A man should be nervous about marrying a treasure like you."

The back door opens and Anne bursts in, her arms full of garment bags and makeup cases. "I know I'm early, but I couldn't wait another minute. Let me see the dress!"

I lift the hanger to show her the simple but elegant cream dress we found at a boutique in Barberville. It's nothing fancy, just a knee-length A-line with three-quarter sleeves and delicate lace detailing, but it makes me feel beautiful.

"Oh, Patty," Anne breathes. "It's perfect. Classic and timeless, and it's so *you*."

"You don't think it's too simple?"

"For a ranch wedding in October? It's absolutely perfect." Anne sets down her bags and pulls out a shoe box. "Speaking of perfect, wait until you see what I found."

She opens the box to reveal a pair of cream-colored flats with tiny pearl buttons. Practical but pretty, comfortable enough to walk on grass but elegant enough for a wedding.

"Anne, they're beautiful. But you didn't need to—"

"Yes, I did. Every bride needs to feel special, and since you insisted on keeping everything low-key, I had to sneak in a surprise somewhere." She grins. "Besides, they're my gift to you. Something new. I know Gabby loaned you her pumps, but she just offered them to see what size you were for me."

Margaret clears her throat. "Speaking of gifts . . ." She disappears into the pantry and emerges with a small wrapped box. "This is something old. It belonged to Finn's grandmother."

I open the box with trembling fingers to find a delicate pearl bracelet. "Oh, it's so . . . perfect. Margaret, I can't take this."

"You're not taking it. It's yours by right. Finn's grandmother wore it on her wedding day, and his mother wore it on hers. It's meant to be passed down to the women who join this family. His mom would have loved to give it to you herself, but..." She trails off. "Anyway, I'm glad to do the honors."

Tears blur my vision as Margaret fastens the bracelet around my wrist. "Thank you."

"Oh, sweetheart." Margaret pulls me into a hug that smells like cinnamon and love. "You've been a gift to this family from the moment you walked into our lives."

Anne, never one to let a sentimental moment pass without commentary, wipes her eyes and claps her hands. "Okay, enough tears before I ruin my makeup. We have a bride to get ready!"

The next few hours pass in a blur of preparation. We push the prep island to one side for space, pull the kitchen curtains closed and lock the door so no one walks in on us. Anne works magic with my hair, creating an elegant updo with small braids woven through it. Margaret helps me into my dress, both of us laughing when I nearly trip over my own feet in my nervousness. Anne applies just enough makeup to enhance my natural features without making me look like someone else.

"Something blue," Anne announces, producing a small blue hair pin in the shape of a forget-me-not. "For remembering this perfect day forever."

When I look in the mirror, I hardly recognize myself. I look radiant. Happy. Like a woman who's chosen love over fear and is about to marry her best friend.

"He's not going to be able to speak when he sees you," Margaret says with satisfaction.

A knock on the door interrupts us. "Ladies?" Uncle Harry's voice calls. "The guests are seated, and I have one very nervous groom asking if it's time yet."

"Five more minutes!" Anne calls back.

I take a deep breath, looking around the kitchen that's become so familiar, so dear to me. In five minutes, I'll walk out there and marry Finn in front of our small group of family and friends. Ms. Daisy and

Ricky from the diner, Anne and Gabby, Ruth, Dorothy, Dr. Waters, a few neighbors, Alec, and the seasonal crew members who've become like family. And Finn's brothers. His sister Holly couldn't make it with such short notice.

"Ready?" Margaret asks, offering me her arm.

"More than ready," I say, and mean it.

We walk outside together, where white chairs are arranged in neat rows facing an arch made of apple branches and late-season flowers. The October afternoon is crisp but sunny, perfect weather for an outdoor wedding. Soft guitar music fills the air, played by one of the crew members who turned out to have hidden talents.

But I only have eyes for Finn.

He's standing at the front in a dark gray suit, his hands clasped behind his back, and when he sees me, his face transforms. The nervous energy melts away, replaced by pure joy and wonder.

Uncle Harry, serving as both father of the bride and officiant (courtesy of an online ordination course he completed last week), meets us halfway down the aisle.

"Who gives this woman to be married?" he asks with a slight smile.

"She gives herself," Margaret says firmly, "with our blessing and our love."

It's the answer we chose together, the one that feels right. I'm not being given away or transferred from one man to another. I'm choosing to join my life with Finn's as an equal partner.

When I reach the front, Finn takes my hands in his, and immediately everything feels right. The nerves fade away until it's just us.

"Hi," he whispers, his eyes bright with unshed tears.

"Hi," I whisper back, squeezing his hands.

Uncle Harry clears his throat and begins the ceremony with words we wrote together, about partnership and choice and building a lasting relationship, together. When it comes time for vows, Finn goes first.

"Patty," he says, his voice steady despite the emotion in his eyes, "when I met you, I didn't know I was looking for someone to complete my life. I thought I had everything figured out. But you showed me the difference between existing and truly living. You taught me that real love isn't about finding someone who fits into your plans, it's about finding someone worth changing your plans for."

My eyes fill with tears, but I manage to keep listening.

"I promise to support your dreams, even when they scare me. I promise to trust your strength, even when my instincts tell me to protect you. I promise to choose you every day, not because I have to, but because I can't imagine choosing anyone else."

When it's my turn, I look into his deep blue eyes and speak from my heart.

"Finn, you helped me see I could trust my judgment about people. You showed me what it feels like to be loved for who I am, not who someone wants me to be. You see my strength instead of my weaknesses, my potential instead of my past."

I take a shaky breath. "I promise to build a life with you based on honesty and respect. I promise to be your partner in all things, your equal in this marriage. I promise to love you not just for who you are today, but for who you're still becoming."

Uncle Harry pronounces us husband and wife, and when Finn kisses me, it feels like a promise being kept. The small crowd cheers, and suddenly we're surrounded by hugs and congratulations and the joyful chaos of celebration.

Through it all, Finn's hand never leaves mine.

Just as Margaret and Anne start ushering guests toward the barn for the reception, a familiar *moo* cuts through the applause.

I glance toward the orchard fence and burst into laughter. Clarabelle, Duchess Mooington herself, is trotting across the lawn with a ribbon tied loosely around one horn and a garland of wilted daisies trailing from her ear. Alec jogs after her, half-laughing, half-scolding, clearly the culprit behind her makeshift accessories.

"She wasn't invited," Margaret mutters, trying not to smile.

"I think she heard there'd be apple pie," Finn says, grinning as Clarabelle makes a beeline for the dessert table.

Before she can get too close, Alec intercepts her and gently nudges her toward the pasture gate. "You already got your invite revoked for licking the wedding cake box this morning," he tells her. Clarabelle lets out a huff of indignation and flicks her tail as if to say she wasn't interested in an invite anyway.

I squeeze Finn's hand, giggling. "That's one way to make the wedding memorable."

"Only fitting," he says. "Our wedding wouldn't be complete without an appearance from the Duchess. I hope the photographer got some pictures of the wedding crasher."

I lean my head against Finn's shoulder as we watch Alec lead Clarabelle back toward the pasture, her floral accessories bouncing with every step.

"Welcome to married life," I murmur.

Finn kisses the top of my head and pulls me a little closer. "If it's anything like today—chaotic, joyful, a little ridiculous—I think we're going to do just fine."

And with that, we walk hand in hand toward the barn, ready to start our forever—with a few hoofprints in the grass and a whole lot of love.

CHAPTER TWENTY-TWO

Finn

P atty wanted to go help Margaret get the food out to the barn, but thankfully Anne commandeered several of the farm hands and my brothers to assist, and made Patty stay with me. We signed the certificate and greeted some guests, and we're sitting outside holding hands, her head resting on my shoulder, when we get word it's time to start. The afternoon sun filters through the apple trees as our small wedding party makes its way from the ceremony site to the barn for supper and the reception. My hand finds Patty's as we walk, and I can't stop looking at the simple gold band on her finger, or the matching one on mine.

"I can't believe we actually did it," she says softly, her white dress rustling as we walk across the grass.

"Any regrets, Mrs. Miller?" I ask, squeezing her hand.

Her smile lights up her entire face. "Only that it took us so long to figure it out."

I look sideways at her and grin. "'Took us so long?' We only dated for two months. You're right, though, sugar. I should have married you on our second date."

She laughs, and I wrap her up in my arms and steal a quick kiss outside the doors to the barn, which has been transformed for the occasion. String lights hang from the rafters, creating a warm glow over the space. Round tables covered with white linens are scattered throughout, each topped with mason jars filled with an assortment of fall flowers. A small area has been cleared for dancing, and someone's set up speakers in the corner.

"Finn! Patty!" Cooper's voice booms across the barn as my brothers approach. They made it just in time for the ceremony, having driven straight through from their respective cities. "Congratulations, you two!"

Colton's right behind him, grinning as he pulls us both into a group hug. "About time you made an honest woman of her," he teases, earning a laugh from Patty.

"Where's Holly?" Alec asks, looking around for my sister.

"Still in New York," Caleb explains with a grimace. "Her program wouldn't let her take time off, but she sends her love. And this." He produces a small wrapped gift. "She made me promise to give you this personally."

Patty tears open the paper to reveal a delicate silver bracelet with a small apple charm. "Oh, it's beautiful. I'll have to call her later to thank her."

"Holly's going to be so mad she missed this," Colton says, shaking his head. "She's been asking for updates on you every week since you met at the diner."

"We'll celebrate with her when she gets back," I say, wrapping my arm around Patty's waist. "Right now, I'm just glad you guys made it."

The small gathering begins to fill the barn. Ms. Daisy and Ricky from the diner, Anne and Gabby, Ruth, and several neighbors all mingle with our ranch family. It's exactly the kind of intimate celebration I'd hoped for.

Uncle Harry taps a spoon against his glass, and the barn gradually quiets. "If I could have everyone's attention," he says, standing near the head table with Margaret beside him. "Margaret and I want to say a few words about our newlyweds."

Margaret takes his hand, her face glowing with happiness. "When Harry and I were planning our own wedding not too long ago, I never imagined we'd be hosting another one so soon. But watching Finn and Patty find each other has been one of the greatest joys of this harvest season."

"Finn," Uncle Harry continues, his voice thick with emotion, "you've grown into the kind of man your father would be proud of, just like I'm proud of you. And Patty, you've brought a joy to this family that we didn't even know we were missing. You've made our boy complete."

There's a chorus of "hear, hear" from the gathered guests, and I feel Patty lean into me, her eyes bright with unshed tears.

"To finding love when you least expect it." Uncle Harry raises his glass. "And to the courage to grab hold of it when you do."

The evening unfolds with the easy warmth of family and friends. Margaret has outdone herself with the food—tender roast, buttery soft rolls, green beans, and mac and cheese that could make anyone weep with joy. Patty and I opted for an apple cake with cream cheese frosting for dessert.

"Everything's delicious," Patty tells Margaret as we sample the food. "Thank you for all your hard work."

"We had fun," Margaret says, nodding toward Anne and Ms. Daisy, who are chatting animatedly at a nearby table. "And it gave me an outlet for my nervous energy. I was almost as anxious as you were."

As the sun sets outside, someone starts the music, and the makeshift dance floor fills with couples. Uncle Harry and Margaret sway together near the center, lost in each other despite the activity around them. They look exactly like the newlyweds they still are.

"Think that'll be us in thirty years?" Patty asks, watching them with a soft smile.

"I do," I say, mimicking our vows from earlier.

As the evening progresses, I find myself watching the interactions around us. Cooper's making everyone laugh with a dramatic retelling of how he had to wrestle a muddy runaway pig during a farm call last week—complete with sound effects and exaggerated gestures—while Colton's helping Mrs. Chen track down her escaped grandson, who's currently hiding under the dessert table with a cookie in each hand. These are good men, my brothers. Men who could help build a legacy here in Piney Brook.

A slow song starts playing, and I turn to Patty. "Care to dance, Mrs. Miller?"

Her smile could light up the whole ranch. "I thought you'd never ask, Mr. Miller."

We move onto the makeshift dance floor, and I pull her close. Around us, other couples sway, their heads craned our direction, faces beaming at us as we dance. I nod at a few of them, then look at Patty with wide eyes.

"You ever feel like you're being watched?" I whisper.

Patty giggles. "Oh, so you're paranoid, hmm? I should have known you were hiding something from me. I hope that doesn't get passed down to our kids."

"Already thinking of kids, huh?"

She's smiling up at me, making my heart smile back. "Yep. Think how great that's going to be. They're going to be beautiful."

"They will be if they look like their mom. They'll just get blue eyes and the paranoia from me."

Patty laughs, and I pick her up and spin us both around and bury my face in her neck. We finish out that song wrapped in each other's arms, but when the next one starts, I just want to be alone with my bride. "Care to take this outside for a minute?" I ask quietly. "I want to show you something."

She nods, and we slip out of the barn into the cool early evening air. The sounds of the reception fade to a gentle murmur behind us as I lead her to the front porch of the farmhouse.

"Look," I say, gesturing toward the view.

From here, we can see the lights of Piney Brook twinkling in the distance, and beyond that, the dark outline of the hills. The orchard spreads out before us, the light of dusk catching on the apple trees we walked through on our second date.

"It's beautiful," Patty says softly, leaning against the porch railing.

"This is what I wanted to show you," I say, moving to stand behind her, my arms circling her waist. "Our life. This view, this land, this community we're now officially part of together."

She leans back against me, and I rest my chin on her shoulder. "I never thought I'd have anything like this," she admits quietly. "A family of my own. Someone who loves me exactly as I am."

"You'll always have it now," I promise, pressing a kiss to her temple. "You'll always have me."

We stand there in comfortable silence, looking out over our new life together. Behind us, I can hear the celebration continuing. Cooper's voice rising above the others as he tells another story. The sound of laughter and clinking glasses.

"Think your brothers will decide to come back?" Patty asks eventually.

"I don't know," I admit. "But I'll love it if they do. This place is big enough for all of us, and there's plenty of work to go around."

"I hope they do come back. I love seeing you with them. I can tell they're your best friends."

"No, *you're* my best friend. You smell better. And you kiss better than them, too." She chuckles as I give her five quick kisses all over her face.

A burst of laughter from inside draws our attention. Through the window, we can see Cooper attempting to show some of the older folks what he calls his "signature dance moves," while Colton looks on with obvious amusement.

"We should probably go rescue them," Patty says, though she doesn't move to leave.

"Probably," I agree, also making no move to go inside. "In a minute."

Because this moment—standing here with my wife on the porch of our new life together, looking out over the land that's been in our family for generations—is perfect. Tomorrow will bring new challenges, new decisions about the ranch and what comes next. But tonight, everything is exactly as it should be.

"Ready to go back to our party, Mrs. Miller?" I ask eventually.

"Ready when you are, Mr. Miller," she replies.

Hand in hand, we head back inside to rejoin our celebration, our family, and our future. Whatever comes next, we'll face it together.

CHAPTER TWENTY-THREE

Epilogue

SIX MONTHS LATER - SPRING

The scent of apple blossoms drifts through the open kitchen window as I roll out pie crust at the farmhouse counter. Outside, the orchard is a symphony of white and pink blooms, exactly as beautiful as Finn promised it would be when we first met. The trees that looked so stark and bare during our first winter together are now bursting with life and possibility.

"That smells incredible," Finn says, appearing in the doorway with dirt on his boots and satisfaction on his face. "What's the occasion?"

"Caleb called," I tell him, crimping the edges of what has become his favorite apple pie. "He's driving down from Missouri this weekend. Says he has something important to discuss."

Finn's eyebrows rise with interest as he washes his hands at the sink. "Important how?"

"He wouldn't say over the phone. Just that it's about his long-term goals." I slide the pie into the oven and set the timer. "But he sounded different. More settled, maybe?"

"Caleb's always been the thoughtful one," Finn muses, drying his hands on the dish towel. "I'm curious what's got him making mysterious phone calls."

I lean against the counter, studying my husband's face. After six months of marriage, I can read his expressions like one of Margaret's well-worn recipe cards. There's hope there, carefully contained but unmistakable.

"You're thinking about the vet clinic idea again, aren't you?" I ask.

Finn's guilty smile gives him away. "Maybe. This area could really use a large-animal vet. Dr. Davis's focus is on small animals, and the nearest large animal veterinarian is an hour away."

"And you think Caleb might be interested?"

"I think Caleb might be exactly what this community needs," Finn says, wrapping his arms around me from behind. "The question is whether he's ready to come home."

The sound of a car on the gravel drive interrupts our conversation. Through the window, I can see a familiar blue SUV pulling up to the house.

"He's early," I say, untying my apron.

"Caleb's always been punctual," Finn replies, but there's nervous energy in his voice now. "Come on, let's go badger the news out of him."

We step onto the front porch just as Caleb emerges from his vehicle.

"There are the newlyweds," he calls, grabbing a duffel bag from the backseat. "Still acting all domestic and disgustingly happy, I see."

"Every day," I laugh, giving him a hug. "How was the drive?"

"Long, but worth it. This place looks incredible in the spring." He gestures toward the blooming orchard, then looks back at us with a grin. "So, ready to hear my news?"

"Yes. Spill it." Finn says.

Caleb sets his bag down on the porch and takes a deep breath. "I've been thinking about what I want to do with my life. About where I want to practice."

"And?" I prompt when he pauses.

"And I want to come home. Not here to the ranch," he adds quickly, holding up a hand as Finn starts to speak. "I think I need my own space. In town."

Finn's face shows a flicker of disappointment before settling into understanding. "That sounds great to me. Piney Brook's not too far of a drive."

"Exactly. I've been doing research. There's a new vet's office on Main Street and the owner, Dr. Davis, is looking for a partner. He's excited about having someone to refer large animal cases to." Caleb's enthusiasm builds as he talks. "I could serve this whole area, from Piney Brook to Barberville and beyond."

"That's wonderful," I say, meaning it completely. "When would you start?"

"I gave my notice already, so . . . in a month or so. I was thinking I could be set up and operational by early fall, just in time for—"

"Breeding season," Finn finishes, his disappointment completely replaced by excitement. "Caleb, that's perfect timing."

"Plus," Caleb adds with a grin, "someone needs to be around to keep an eye on Cooper when he finally decides to come back too."

"Cooper's coming back?" I ask, surprised.

"He's thinking about it." Caleb shrugs. "Though knowing Cooper, he'll probably want to turn the ranch into some kind of vacation work-farm destination."

Finn and I exchange a look. The idea isn't entirely without merit.

"So, now that we've got that settled, let's eat." Caleb picks up his bag again. "Speaking of settled, can you believe how well Uncle Harry and Margaret are doing in their new place?" he asks as we head inside.

"I'm loving the updates," I reply. "Did you check the chat yet today?"

"Not yet."

"Margaret sent pictures of their little cottage. It's right on the water, and Harry's already talking about getting a fishing boat."

"Nice. They earned it," Finn says. "Forty years of running this place, they deserve to relax and enjoy themselves."

"And you two are doing okay managing everything on your own?"

I look at my husband, thinking about the challenges and triumphs of our first winter and spring together. The burst pipe that flooded the mudroom in January, the late frost that threatened the apple blossoms, the pure joy of watching our first crop emerge from the soil we'd planted together.

"More than okay," I say. "We're actually thinking about expanding the vegetable garden this year. Maybe selling at the farmer's market in Barberville."

"Look at you, becoming a real farm wife," Caleb teases, but his tone is affectionate.

"Look at you, coming home to join a veterinary practice," I counter. "Who would've thought the Miller boys would all end up back where they started?"

"Not all of us," Finn points out. "Yet."

"Give it time," Caleb says confidently. "This place has a way of calling its people home when they're ready."

That evening, we sit on the front porch watching the sunset paint the apple blossoms in shades of gold and pink. Caleb's telling us about his plans for expanding the services at the clinic, his voice full of the kind of passion that comes from finding your purpose.

"Have you told Cooper about your decision?" Finn asks.

"I called him this morning. He's excited. Says it gives him another reason to visit." Caleb takes a sip of the sweet tea I made. "He might actually drive down next month to look around."

"What made you decide to come back?" I ask Caleb.

He's quiet for a long moment, looking out over the land his great-grandfather settled. "I realized that all the things I thought I wanted didn't matter if I wasn't happy. And when I thought about where I felt most happy, it was always here. Maybe not on this exact piece of land, but in this community."

"Plus," he adds with a grin, "someone needs to keep Finn from thinking he can doctor his own animals when they get sick."

"That was one time," Finn protests. "And the calf was fine."

"The calf was *lucky*," Caleb corrects, making us all laugh.

As the stars begin to appear overhead, I think about the changes this past year has brought. A husband who loves me exactly as I am. A home where I feel safe and valued. And now, potentially, more family settling nearby.

A year ago, I was running from a life that nearly destroyed me. Now I'm building a beautiful home with people who've become my chosen family.

"Thank you," I say quietly to both brothers.

"For what?" Caleb asks.

"For making me feel like I belong."

Finn reaches over and takes my hand. "You do belong. This is your home now too."

"Our home," I correct, squeezing his fingers. "All of ours."

And looking out over the apple blossoms glowing in the moonlight, I know that whatever challenges and changes lie ahead, we'll face them together. As a family.

Wow, what a journey Patty and Finn have been on. I hope you loved their story as much as I do!

If you enjoyed the story, I'd love it if you'd consider leaving a review. Even a star rating helps other readers find my stories. Click here to leave a review. https://www.amazon.com/dp/B0F1L6X5LV/

Curious what happens when Cooper decides to put down roots at the ranch? Find out in His to Hold.

https://www.amazon.com/gp/product/B0FCD29L8R

That's not it for Finn and Patty, though. Find out what their life looks like two years from now in the Bonus Epilogue, exclusive to newsletter subscribers. Get it here: https://BookHip.com/JQQRCZD

Also By Tia Marlee

Piney Brook Wishes Series

His Christmas Wish

Sweet Summertime Wishes

Wishing for the Girl Next Door

A Soldier's Wish

Her New Year's Wish

The Piney Brook Wishes Box Set

The Coffee Loft Series

Bean Wishing for a Latte Love

You Mocha Me Crazy

A Brewtiful Kind of Love

Coffee Loft Collection

Apple Blossom Ranch Series

His to Adore
His to Have
His to Hold
His to Love
His to Cherish
Hers to Treasure

Sugar and Sirens
Still Yours, Always Mine
Catch Me, If You Can
Sweeter With You
A Little Bit Married
The Last First Kiss

A Cobb County Christmas
Merry & Bright: The Great Light Fight
Gnome Sweet Home
The Candy Cane Parade

Let's Stay In Touch

You can find me at my website: https://tiamarlee.com

Follow me:

Facebook: https://tinyurl.com/FBTiaMarlee

Instagram: https://tinyurl.com/IGTiaMarlee

Amazon: https://tinyurl.com/AmazonTiaMarlee

BookBub: https://tinyurl.com/BBTiaMarlee

Goodreads: https://tinyurl.com/GRTiaMarlee

Join my reader group: https://tinyurl.com/TiaMarleeReaderGroup

About Tia

Tia Marlee resides in Central Texas with her husband and three teenage children. When she isn't writing, Tia enjoys reading, embroidery and spending time with her family. Tia is the author of sweet, no-steam, small-town, contemporary romance stories. Her books are like Hallmark meets real life with a dash of humor.

Follow Tia on Facebook, Instagram, or check out her website for more information.

www.ingramcontent.com/pod-product-compliance
Lightning Source LLC
Chambersburg PA
CBHW032005240626
47153CB00003B/1132